STÉPHANE CARLIER grew up around Paris in the 1970s. He worked for the French Ministry for Europe and Foreign Affairs for several years, with whom he spent a decade in the United States. He has also lived in India and Portugal. *Clara Reads Proust* is his eighth novel and the first to be translated into English.

POLLY MACKINTOSH is an editor and a translator from French. She has translated the work of Alain Ducasse, Antoine Laurain, Serge Joncour and early French feminist Marie-Louise Gagneur. She currently lives in London.

A Gallic Book

First published in France as *Clara lit Proust*
by Éditions Gallimard, 2022
© Éditions Gallimard, Paris, 2022

English translation copyright © Gallic Books, 2024

All quotations from *À la recherche du temps perdu*
by Marcel Proust are from the C. K. Scott Moncrieff translations:
Swann's Way (1922),
Within a Budding Grove (1924),
The Guermantes Way (1925)

First published in Great Britain in 2023 by
Gallic Books, 12 Eccleston Street, London, SW1W 9LT

A CIP record for this book is available from the British Library

ISBN 978-1-913547-73-8

Typeset in Garamond by Gallic Books
Printed and bound in the UK by CPI (CR0 4YY)

2 4 6 8 10 9 7 5 3 1

CLARA READS PROUST

STÉPHANE CARLIER
Translated by Polly Mackintosh

Gallic Books
London

For my brother, Raphaël,
a light in the dark

The thing is to free one's self: to let it find its dimensions, not be impeded.

VIRGINIA WOOLF

I

CINDY COIFFURE

Madame Habib is standing on the pavement, wearing a blouse despite the cold, one arm extended to keep her cigarette at a distance, while the other remains folded across her stomach. Stiff and shivering, she examines the window of her salon as if she is trying to solve its mystery. There's the white lettering of the logo, the huge poster of a woman with Louise Brooks–style hair who looks like she's staring at her feet, the price list on the glass door. And, at the other end, right at the bottom, lonely and useless in its see-through vase, there's a stalk of bamboo which has never grown more than a centimetre.

'The problem is the name. That's what the previous owner's daughter was called. It was all the rage back in 1982, but it doesn't mean anything to anyone now.'

Madame Habib is completely wrong about her salon's reputation. She has daydreamed about it so much that she has convinced herself she's running an elite salon, while in actual fact Cindy Coiffure is tiny, both long and narrow, hidden in a nook that is itself hidden down a passage, and only survives thanks to a customer base of loyal regulars, whose average age is seventy. Cindy Coiffure is the perfect name for it.

'And don't tell me it should be something to do with "hair". "Hair Today, Gone Tomorrow", or whatever. I hate puns.' She takes a drag on her cigarette, and Clara hears it crackle. 'I've got an idea; tell me what you think.' Short pause for dramatic effect. 'The Garden of Delights.'

She's always struggled with names. Starting with her own. She's never forgiven her husband for giving her a surname that hurts her ears, especially when her maiden name was Delage. *You can say what you want, but Jacqueline Delage still sounds better than Jacqueline Habib.*

'What does it make you think of?'

A Chinese restaurant, Clara wants to say, but instead she just shrugs her shoulders. It doesn't matter. If it wasn't the name of the salon, then it would be that the façade needed repainting or that they should start doing manicures. *(There are always loads of people at The Nail Shop on Rue Thiers, have you noticed?)*

She knows what's going to happen. Madame Habib will take one final puff on her cigarette, blow out the smoke as far as she can while she crushes the butt under her left foot, then she'll say something like *At least we won't die of heat today* and go back inside. In the back room, she'll wash her hands and have a mint. She'll come back into view, looking at herself in a mirror, then she'll go back to the till, smoothing down her skirt. Someone will come in, the salon will come to life with the sound of murmured conversation, whirring hairdryers and the old hits on Radio Nostalgie, and it will be as though none of it had ever happened – The Garden of Delights, puns on 'hair' and names that were all the rage back in 1982.

Lorraine is usually the first to arrive. The minute the salon opens, she shows up with two coffees on a little round tray and sits down on the high stool by the till to have a gossip with Madame Habib.

She runs the café on the corner between the passage and Avenue de la Libération. By the time she gets to the salon, she's already been on her feet for several hours and can't stand it any longer. Her customers drive her mad: the blokes who need their Calvados at eight in the morning and talk to her as if she's their wife or sister; the down-and-outs who spend their benefits on the lottery, their coins scraping against the table as they scratch their cards; the embarrassed smokers – *I'll have a pack of Dunhills – it's been years* . . . Jacqueline listens, remaining so perfectly still that from behind, it looks like she's asleep standing up. She goes to visit Lorraine on her breaks too, but later in the day and less frequently. She usually comes back humming and smelling of brandy.

Often Lorraine will say, *I'd rather have hung myself than go to work this morning.* She counts down the days until her next holiday and is transformed as it draws nearer. When she comes to the salon for a cut and colour just before leaving, she's a new woman – she's like her own twin sister, full of the joys of life. She'll come back from her holiday crimson and a little plumper, her hair lighter still. She'll remain in good spirits and talk about signing up for tai chi and getting back into photography – *I really mean it this time.* Then she'll talk about that less and less and, shortly before autumn officially begins, when the last of her tan has faded, those familiar words will return to her lips: *I'd rather have hung myself than go to work this morning.*

In her salon at nine in the morning, Madame Habib looks more like a woman playing at the casino on a Saturday night. A Havana-brown or leopard-print silk shirt, bracelets that clink together at the slightest movement, and Shalimar, lots of Shalimar, so much Shalimar that the perfume permeates the whole room and has become as much a part of it as the white marble-effect tiles and the two chiming notes of the doorbell at the entrance. Her heavy makeup accentuates the tiredness in her eyes, which bulge slightly out of her head. Her cigarette-damaged voice is hoarse, just like it is at the end of a long, quiet day without any customers. Her complexion is dark brown from powder, as well as from sessions on the tanning bed – Madame Habib is a tanoholic (on a nice day, it is not uncommon to spot her in Place de la Libération on her lunch break, perched at the end of a bench not yet in the shade, eating her rice salad with her face turned towards the sun).

On Tuesday mornings, Clara will often wonder how she spent the preceding two days. They don't talk about it – they aren't close enough for that kind of thing. It is only through listening to what Madame Habib has told her customers over time that Clara has been able to figure out who her boss really is.

There was indeed a Monsieur Habib, transmitter of the despised surname, who, for one reason or another, is no longer around – whether he died or just left, Clara isn't sure. That is the greatest taboo of all. There is a daughter, a nurse who lives near Toulon, whom Madame Habib sees once or twice a year and whom she doesn't seem to care for all that much. There is Paris – ah, Paris! Madame Habib lived there once, and it is one subject that she is more than happy to talk about. She always tells the same stories: that she could see the dome of the Panthéon from her kitchen window; that an actor whose name Clara has forgotten used to leave roses on her doormat on his way to the theatre; that Parisians are intelligent, cultured, that every one of them reads. *Even the layabouts on the métro have a book in their hands.* Perhaps that's the reason for the lines that etch brackets on either side of her mouth: regret that she no longer lives in the city where she was happiest.

Layabout is a word she is particularly fond of. As is the expression *don't get your knickers in a knot. Don't get your knickers in a knot, but we've run out of hairspray, I don't know how this has happened.* And she uses the English term *nail salon* instead of the French *manucure*, pronouncing it the English way. *One of my daughter's friends has opened a 'nail salon' in Hyères that's a runaway success,* she would announce, waiting for her interlocutor to be impressed by the expression.

Besides, there were rumours. A few years ago, she was apparently seen walking across a rapeseed field on the outskirts of Beaune, her Mini Mayfair parked at the roadside a little further down. It was said that she was drunk. It was also said that when she first arrived in the area, before she took over the salon, she dated the man who was at the time the mayor of Dijon.

She loves men – of that, Clara is sure. You can tell from the way she looks at the few who come into the salon and from the way she speaks to them, whether they are handsome or ugly, young or old, wearing overalls or Havaiana flip-flops. And from the way she talks about JB. JB is Clara's boyfriend. He is also the only personal matter that Madame Habib discusses with her employee – or rather, the only one she can't help herself from discussing. It's been that way since the beginning, since the first time he came to see Clara at Cindy Coiffure. Jacqueline couldn't stand still; her lips were quivering with emotion. You could tell she was upset that she hadn't been warned, that she hadn't had time to top up her makeup. She'd acted as if she was their age, as if she'd been in line for JB's affections before Clara. It was absurd, like a bad amateur dramatics production. JB gave Clara a questioning look. Clara wanted to reassure her boss and tell her that everything was fine, that it wasn't a competition and there was no need to panic.

A few days went by, and then, one evening at closing time, Madame Habib said: *If I had a man like that in my life, I wouldn't give a damn about the salon. In fact, I don't think I'd work at all. I'd spend my time cooking and looking after our apartment. Anything to make sure he didn't leave.*

Before she picks up the phone, Madame Habib removes the earring from her right earlobe. Then she says, *Bonjour, Cindy Coiffure, Jacqueline speaking*, all in one breath, her eyes fixed on the glass door even though there's no one there, weighing up her earring in her left hand as if it were a marble.

Then there's Nolwenn, the salon's other employee. Her face is almost without contours and her expression rarely changes. Whether she's talking about her sister-in-law's miscarriage or giving Clara a birthday present, her features remain neutral. The only time they come to life is when she's watching videos on her phone. The bottom half of her face will break into a huge smile at the sight of a chimpanzee walking a piglet on a lead, or a golden retriever trying to climb the first step of a staircase. She used to show Clara these videos before finally giving up, obviously disappointed at her lack of reaction. Now she no longer shares them, and on her breaks, she can often be heard chuckling alone in the courtyard behind the salon.

She says things like *It'll be OK there* (instead of *It'll be OK* – the *there* doesn't refer to anything), *We've been at sixes and sevens this week* (when it's been particularly busy at the salon) and *stubborn hair*, which she has used at every opportunity since recently hearing it. Sometimes she even uses two of these expressions in the same sentence: *I didn't think straightening would work for Madame Rinaldi's stubborn hair, but it'll be OK there.*

Nolwenn hasn't always got on well with her boss. At the beginning, they didn't get on at all. *She doesn't have the eye for it*, Madame Habib would say, needing to go out for a cigarette to calm down after watching her at work, or worse, take over from Nolwenn mid-snip. The way she held herself, the impression of sluggishness she gave off was also a problem. *Come on, get up! You're like a cow watching a train go by!* It seemed obvious she wasn't going to last long. But Nolwenn is tough, tougher than she looks. She listened to Jacqueline's comments and, without showing that they'd affected her, she tried again, re-did a customer's curls, repeated to herself the name or quantity of a certain product. This silent determination must have made an impression on Madame Habib, and she kept her on, against all odds. Things are better nowadays. Nolwenn still sits down whenever she has the chance and she's always in a rush to leave the salon (at seven o'clock on the dot she's practically running out of the door), but she no longer makes basic errors and she covers her mouth when she yawns. Madame Habib still keeps an eye on her and has to lecture her sometimes (*Have some class, would you!*), but her tone is different now. Nolwenn has found her niche at Cindy Coiffure, to the point that she feels at home – perhaps more so here than anywhere else. It's as though time has brought about a sort of symbiosis between the simple, modest place and the young woman who embodies it.

Nolwenn once came back from her leave with a perm. She'd had it cut into a bob. It's a style that doesn't suit anyone, and it certainly didn't suit her. Her large face flanked with ringlets which shook at the slightest movement – it was a disaster. The customers paused for a moment as they took it in; a few of them looked at Madame Habib questioningly. (Did she lose a bet? Is it Halloween already?) Jacqueline didn't say a word. It must have seemed like a particularly long day to Nolwenn, who returned the next day with her hair straightened again.

There's Patrick, too. He only works on Saturdays and over holidays like Easter, All Saints' Day and Christmas, when you'll see him every day. Patrick is the jewel in Cindy Coiffure's crown. 'He's really an exceptional hairdresser,' Madame Habib repeats ad infinitum. 'He'll have his own salon in Dijon one day, or maybe even in Lyon.'

He's a rather large man, and not always impeccably turned out. His life doesn't seem easy – he is separated from the mother of his son, and he doesn't see him as often as he would like. He is always calculating something or other – the price of haircuts, the quantity of tips, the number of hours worked – and he loses his temper easily. He once called Madame Garcin an *old bat*. Madame Habib forced him to apologise, which he did, and Madame Garcin claimed she wasn't offended, but she never came back.

Clara thinks he could at least smile a little more. Jacqueline must think the same thing, but she doesn't say anything. Just as she keeps to herself her thoughts on his tardiness and bitten-down nails, and on the black T-shirts that hang free from his trousers. She's too afraid she'd lose him. But she isn't quite the same on the days when he's working. She becomes tense, she talks less, and she surreptitiously watches him to make sure everything is alright. She knows Patrick is responsible for what little reputation her salon has. Some customers come all the way from Lons to have their hair done by him. Clara is good and the customers like her, but they wouldn't drive an hour and a half to see her.

Patrick likes Clara too. She is one of the few women at Cindy Coiffure who doesn't make him feel sad. He once showed her some drawings on his phone, some black-and-white manga-style cartoons, both erotic and violent. She was impressed – did he really draw them? He'd also tried to convert her to Rage Against the Machine, the greatest metal band of all time in his eyes, but she couldn't really get into them.

One Saturday when he had back-to-back appointments, he announced that he wasn't going to *rot in this hole*, as he took a drag on a roll-up cigarette in the courtyard behind the salon between customers. It was summer, the air conditioning was broken and everyone inside was suffocating. *And you aren't either*, he added. She would have liked him to elaborate, but he crushed his cigarette against the wall and went back to work.

Madame Habib worships Jacques Chirac. According to her, France has never been so great as it was when he presided over it, and things all started to go wrong afterwards. She worships him to the extent that she has pinned a photo of him to the wall near the till, a little black-and-white photo cut from a magazine in which he is barely recognisable – he looks more like an actor from Hollywood's Golden Age. She explains it to the few customers who are still new to the picture: *With that physique, what do you expect?* Meaning: when you are that attractive, you are destined only for great things.

JB makes everyone swoon. Clara's customers, her friends, her sister. Even her parents, who aren't at all the type to gush, feel the need to express their feelings. *You've always been lucky, ever since you were little* (her mother). *If you're not getting married because of the money, we can help* (her father).

He does tick all the boxes. Physically, he resembles Flynn Rider from *Tangled*, the Disney animation. Like Flynn, he has black hair that flops down into his eyes, the build of an American football player and a penchant for practical jokes (making people smear shaving cream on their nose, turning up to parties in fancy dress – that sort of thing). His skin shows no sign of age or hardship, and people are constantly telling him so. He is a firefighter, a job that all young boys dream of, and he even goes into schools to talk about it. He excels in an impressive number of sports, including football, volleyball and motocross, and he can hold his own at tennis. He is attentive and considerate, and never forgets to buy Clara flowers or organise a surprise birthday party for her on the twenty-ninth of March.

At least, that's what other people see. That's what Clara saw too, at the beginning of their relationship. Now, almost three years after their first date, what she sees most of the time is a man with weaknesses. A man who stands by the living room window on some mornings, bowl of Chocapic in hand, with an air of great sorrow. A man who drinks a little too much the night before his days off, who hardly speaks to his father and sometimes has fights in his sleep, spewing terrible insults. A man she no longer desires. There you have it, the stubborn little cloud on the horizon of her existence. Her Flynn Rider, the mere mention of whom would once send shivers all the way down to her little toe, is now as tempting as a plate of cold meats after the Christmas turkey. She looks at his mouth and the corner that tends to rise of its own accord, the light brown of his eyes and the bounce of his hair, and she feels nothing. *Nada, niente, nichts*, as Madame Habib would say.

She thinks about this while she's on the bus to the salon. She remembers them exchanging texts at this time of day when they first started going out. They had just said goodbye, they had slept together, and they were both satisfied, but they still desired one another. So they would call one another, not to talk about anything in particular. Clara would turn to face the window and listen to JB telling her about an early morning dream or listing all the places he wanted to kiss her, in a voice still heavy with sleep. And, since this was never enough, they would also send each other messages, or photos of certain parts of their bodies. Clara liked the flat part just below his neck. She loved placing her hand there; the skin was soft and silky from the hair that covered it. JB would take a photo of that before getting in the shower, and he would send it to her to lift her spirits. It worked: knowing that she had a photo of her boyfriend's sternum on her phone helped her get through the day.

It makes no sense to her now. Thinking back to it is like hearing someone speak in a language she no longer understands. When she's on the bus she'll send a message to her mother or talk to her sister and then she'll scroll on Instagram for a while, closing it before she's seen all the new posts on her feed. She still turns to face the window, but now she thinks about the dwindling of desire and about her physical interactions with JB, which nowadays go no further than a kiss on the lips (sometimes) or on the forehead (increasingly frequently). She thinks to herself that they will soon be like brother and sister. And then she arrives at Place de la Libération.

She doesn't understand why most people find cats fascinating. There's nothing fascinating about hers. He's a big white ball of fur who bolts as soon as anyone tries to stroke him, and, after eleven months of communal life, hisses at his owners in the hallway. His other personality traits, as far as Clara can see, are gluttony (he is overweight), laziness and sadness. His only positive attribute is how photogenic he is, which is useless because his owners are the only people who ever see him. Whenever a guest sets foot in the apartment, he'll run off to one of his hiding places and stay there until the following day, or sometimes even the day after that. *He has a strong personality*, says JB by way of excuse, which infuriates Clara. He does not have a strong personality. He must have once been abused or had a fall from the third floor of a building, perhaps both, making him at once unhappy and deeply unpleasant.

'Come on, this time it's in the bag, eh!'

Madame Habib is speaking to Nolwenn, who is about to take her driving test. She places her hands on Nolwenn's shoulders, forcing her to stand up straight, encouraging her to believe in herself and to crack a smile. It's like watching a coach training a boxer. This is Nolwenn's fifth attempt, and if she fails again, she'll have to *start all over again*, meaning she'll have to do her theory test again too. Last time she got an insane examiner who told her that aeroplane contrails were messages written in the sky by members of a satanic global elite (or something like that). The time before that, the examiner was all there but Nolwenn had forgotten her ID card.

It's a gloomy start to the day at Cindy Coiffure, where every hour feels like an endurance test. Outside, the weather is Scottish: rainy, windy and dark. Inside, it isn't much better. Nolwenn has failed her driving test (she hit a recycling bin trying to parallel park) and, for some reason, the lights in the little glass cabinet that arrived the previous month are no longer working. Madame Habib adores the display case, which she ordered from a catalogue – in her opinion, it makes the salon even classier. She was like a kid on Christmas morning on the day it was delivered, clapping when the technician turned its lights on, and for a week, she said to every customer who came through the door: *Notice anything different?* This morning she's not even bothering to put up a front. Nobody hears a peep from her, except for when she comes out of the back room at the stroke of ten, having turned off 'J'ai encore rêvé d'elle' mid-song, sighing *Thank God that wailing's over.*

Raymonde's Story

It's six thirty and I leave the house to go and see my sister. I wait and wait at the bus station – no bus. Well, yes, the bus is right there in front of me, but we can't get on – there's no driver. The station is closed at this time, so I have to wait to speak to another driver to find out what's going on. Dédé had a seizure as he was leaving the house, he tells me, the bus to Nuits is cancelled. Poor Dédé, I think. Oh well, I'll go tomorrow. And I go home. When I get there, I call my sister and make myself a quick meal. René told me he was spending the evening at boules. He takes the opportunity to play boules when I go and visit Geneviève. So, I eat something, I take the stems off some beans, I take down the washing. After that I've got to sit down 'cos of my legs. I lie on the bed and, of course, I fall asleep. After a while I feel the bed starting to pitch like a boat and I can hear creaking. I still have the strangest dreams, I think to myself as I'm waking up. Except it's not a dream. I turn on the light and what do I see? Some woman in my bed! Some woman doing it with my René! She's on all fours, arse in the air, and he's on his knees, going at it from behind (sorry to be crude, Jacqueline, but that's what happened). I don't know where this woman comes from – she looks Chinese or something, wearing lots of lipstick. When she sees me, she starts wailing like a pig and jumps off the bed and tries to leave while putting her knickers back on. But she can't really manage it and she falls flat on her face in the bedroom. And then, get this: René asks if she's OK. She doesn't reply – she just gets up and leaves, hopping on one leg because she's still putting her knickers back on. What on earth is going on? I ask René, who's getting dressed again. And d'you know what he says? You're not at Geneviève's? That's all he has to say! Honestly, I swear . . . They thought they were home alone. They obviously didn't see me because it was dark. René attempted to explain, but I didn't want to know. I kicked him out. Go and find your Chinese lover! I couldn't even look him in the eye. He didn't argue. I left his stuff on the landing, and he took it bit by bit. He didn't say much, he was in shock as well, it was quite a surprise to find me in the bed . . . I couldn't go back to our bedroom – I slept in Francine's. Well, I didn't sleep very much. I couldn't stop thinking about what had happened. I wondered where René was spending the night, especially 'cos it was raining. I told myself he'd go back to his mother's, but I didn't hear the car or the garage door. And this morning, I could see through the kitchen window that the door of the shed at the end of the garden was ajar. He'd slept in there.

For several days, Lorraine has been complaining about extraordinary dizzy spells that make her feel as though she's in a lift that's plummeting in freefall. *I've never experienced anything so horrible. Every time it happens, I want to die.* Madame Habib listens without batting an eyelid, both because she is interested and because she is a terrible insomniac who feels suddenly exhausted just after opening the salon – to the point that she often has to tap her foot to avoid falling asleep while she's listening to her friend. *How awful*, she replies. And then, because Lorraine doesn't say anything else, because long silences are never good and because it's something that's been on her mind, she follows up with: *People hate the colour pink – I don't think it's fair. An old rose can be very beautiful in a bedroom, say.*

He came to Cindy Coiffure several days in a row. A short man with white hair, wearing a beige overcoat. He would arrive, give Madame Habib a kiss on the cheek, greet Nolwenn and Clara with a nod and then sit down in one of the chairs that's on the right as you come in. He would watch what was going on in the salon, lost in thought. Sometimes he would pick up a magazine and flick through it before quickly putting it down again. His name was never in the appointments book, and he wasn't getting his hair cut, so what was he doing there? Madame Habib's discomfort in his presence put people off asking. After a while, when they'd almost forgotten about him, he would quietly sneak out.

It happened three or four times. Then, one day, Jacqueline saw him approaching and went out to meet him.

'Right, enough is enough, Roger!'

He immediately turned around, and they never saw him again.

It's a Saturday and Patrick hasn't turned up. Madame Gobineau, his first appointment of the day, has been waiting for half an hour in a kind of stupor, as if someone had just told her the exact date of the end of the world. The thirty minutes of non-stop Radio Nostalgie are obviously no longer relaxing her.

By the time his second appointment, Madame Berrada, gets there, thunder is rumbling, it's as dark as if it were six in the evening, and Patrick still hasn't shown up. Madame Habib decides to call him. It goes to voicemail, and she leaves a message that no one will be able to hear because of the racket that Nolwenn's hairdryer is making. She puts the phone down, glances at the sliver of purple sky that can be seen from the salon and offers to do Madame Gobineau's hair herself. Madame Gobineau decides to leave – she's got to call in on the butcher at the market, from whom she has ordered some veal liver; she doesn't really want to go there before she's had her hair done but she doesn't complain, certain that something must have happened to her favourite hairdresser.

It's almost eleven when Patrick finally shows up. He's had

35

his son staying with him since yesterday and his ex has only just picked him up. *It was either that or I brought him with me.*

Clara doesn't quite believe him. Firstly, he looks after his son on Sundays, never on Friday. He also stinks of cigarettes and Red Bull and is clearly wearing last night's clothes. She is almost certain that he has come straight from Hangar, a club in Chenôve that he often talks about and where he must have spent the night.

He gets to work immediately, with the kind of excess energy born of all-nighters. Madame Habib watches him working wonders on Madame Berrada, who is telling him about the food at her daughter's upcoming wedding in minute detail, apparently unperturbed by the state of her hairdresser. Patrick is very lucky. His boss will make a comment as a matter of principle, but it will be so gentle that it is practically a compliment.

Later on, since it's a Saturday and they're running behind schedule, Jacqueline takes off her bracelets, rolls up the sleeves of her camel-coloured blouse and tends to Madame Rousseau's shampoo and set, something she wouldn't usually do. She is feeling relieved after the earlier worry about her employee, and now that everything is back to normal after a brush with disaster, she begins to talk. Clara hears her saying that she used to go to a club in Paris where you would meet *loads of stars*. She had danced with a certain Jacques Chazot there, who told her how beautiful she was before whispering *Paris is your oyster* in her ear . . . Jacqueline, who had frozen after placing the last roller on top of Madame Rousseau's head, suddenly remembers where she is. *Ah, best not go down memory lane.*

Wednesday, 14 August. There aren't any names in the appointment book. Tomorrow, the salon closes for two weeks. Clara was playing Candy Crush, got bored and is now doing a quiz she found in an old copy of *Elle*: *Do you know how to boost your powers of seduction?* An activity that is completely pointless, because not only does she not care about the answer to a question she has never even thought about, but the page of answers is also missing, no doubt ripped out by a customer planning to read it at home.

Two screeching swallows fly past the salon. Nolwenn and Patrick are on holiday. Madame Habib has gone out to buy cigarettes. The only vaguely useful thing she and Clara have done all morning was to look for the best place to put a postcard from Patrick, which they received yesterday. It's a postcard from the Festival des Vieilles Charrues, written partially in Breton, which they placed in the end on the counter against the wall, underneath the photo of Jacques Chirac. Oh, it won't stay there. Maybe a few weeks at most, after which it will end up in the counter drawer among the small change, till roll and business cards of passing salespeople, and then it will quietly disappear.

Madame Habib comes back humming 'Le Sud', which she heard earlier on Radio Nostalgie. Sweat is painting brown haloes on her beige blouse. She puts the cigarettes away in her silver case and disappears into the back room, where Clara can hear her brushing her teeth. Then there's a silence, which is slowly filled by the soft sound of snoring. It stops, and Jacqueline re-emerges shortly afterwards and joins Clara, who is sitting behind the till where the air-con can reach her. Her boss watches her scrolling through the photos on her phone for a few seconds before saying: *If you want to leave, go ahead. I think that's it for today.*

Going for lunch at her parents' house makes her increasingly confused. It's a mixture of anxiety and comfort, of watered-down anxiety – it is very strange. They go there regularly – on Sundays, at midday. Time seems to stretch out when they are there, as if the Earth were deliberately moving more slowly between the hours of 11:30 a.m. and 6 p.m. on that day. Then there's the white light that comes through the net curtains of the living room windows, the pompommed ties that hold back the wall hangings, the chicken and green bean dish that her mother has made them, its smell wafting from the kitchen into other rooms and mingling with the smell of clean laundry and furniture polish. She is moved by all of it, both comforted and saddened, every time. It's as if she is only just discovering it, when in fact it is something that she has always known because it's where she grew up.

The biggest challenge is the walk after the meal, along the flat road next to the fields in the area around the village. The light is always too bright. Clara walks ahead of her parents as their conversation with JB slows. They even stop talking at points. These pauses irritate her just as much as their displays of affection towards a man they would so love to permanently welcome into their family. Her mother's look of contentment, her father's stupid questions (*Do firefighters smoke?*), and JB between the two of them like a pig in muck. He's always said to Clara: *You're so lucky to have them as parents. Mine aren't like that at all.*

Thinking about it has helped her understand at last. Well, to at least come close to something resembling an explanation. She realises it one Sunday evening when she's on the way home, while on the horizon the clearing skies are drenching the Saône-et-Loire countryside in gold. At the root of her distress are several questions. *Is this as good as it gets? Are we as happy as we'll ever be?*

At the salon, a visit from Audrey, a former employee who's come in to introduce her baby, who was born the previous week. Malo, seven pounds one ounce at birth. *A little Leo, like his father*, says Audrey. And: *I didn't feel him coming like I did with Elliot.* Yes, he's her second since she left Cindy Coiffure. Clara, who is in her element, strokes the tiny baby's stomach with her index finger. Nolwenn, who was hired after Audrey left, is less forthcoming. And although Madame Habib is still fond of her ex-employee, she has never been good with children, and certainly not with newborns. Audrey and her pram are hardly out of the door when you hear Jacqueline mutter: *Well, at that age they're nothing but a pipe. What goes in one end comes out the other.*

'You're hurting me!'

Nolwenn has pulled out a lock of Madame Quintin's hair while removing her rollers. What makes it even less understandable is that this is practically the only thing she does: perms and shampoo and sets.

It hasn't escaped Madame Habib's notice. *Go to Mariella Brunella if you want to mess around! They'll take you in with open arms!* Mariella Brunella is the name of a salon in the shopping arcade at Carrefour. Madame Habib loathes it; in her eyes it is the worst place possible to get your hair done, and in fact the worst place full stop – even though it is often full and does a lot better than Cindy Coiffure, attracting a younger, more diverse mix of customers.

Nolwenn apologised to Madame Quintin, but her expression remained neutral, making it look like she didn't mean a word of it.

The technician who has come to repair the display cabinet was well worth the ten-week wait. He is magnificent, a kind of perfection. Henry Cavill, thinks Clara. Nino Castelnuovo, muses Madame Habib. He is charming, with brown hair and the shoulders of a swimmer, and there's a poise, a suppleness to his gestures. It makes you wonder what he's doing repairing display cabinets in Saône-et-Loire instead of walking the catwalk in Paris or Milan. The scene at Cindy Coiffure just before lunch is a sight to behold, the five women in the salon practically rooted to the spot as they watch him crouch, kneel and then lie down on the tiles, contorting his body to get his hand underneath the cabinet, which he repaired far too quickly. *It was a problem with the socket*, he explains. *I've replaced it.* A good reason to put the old one back in and get him to return.

'I have an appointment at eleven,' she said, taking off her coat. 'Under the name Claudie.'

Clara couldn't help but smile. But Madame Habib understood. She shook her head to demonstrate that the clarification wasn't necessary, offered to take the woman's coat with the hurried air of someone who is used to managing sensitive situations, then gestured towards one of the chairs near the entrance. 'Clara is finishing up with Madame Weil and then she'll take care of you.'

Claudie went to sit down as Radio Nostalgie played Cyndi Lauper's 'True Colors', a scheduling coincidence that none of the women in the salon were calm enough to notice. Jacqueline went back to cleaning the display unit on the counter as if nothing out of the ordinary had happened. Clara frowned as she took out Madame Weil's rollers, feeling ashamed of her stupid smile. Meanwhile, Madame Weil was staring into space, with eyes like a greyhound and a look of astonishment on her face. You could practically hear her thinking: *Will someone please tell me what on earth is going on?!*

The school bus driver at Romain-Rolland had become a

woman. Or rather, Claudie Hansen had become herself, having been lost in the body of Claude for over fifty years. She explained this to Madame Habib, Clara and Nolwenn after Madame Weil left. Nolwenn had just got back from her driving lesson and was staring at her as if she'd just seen the WWI soldier from the war memorial on Place de la Libération come to life.

Claudie was in the final stages of transitioning, something she'd wanted to do slowly and gradually to spare herself any unnecessary suffering. First, she'd grown out her hair (*I looked like a musketeer*) before starting to wear heels (*They're the hardest because it leaves no shadow of a doubt*) and then women's clothing. Jewellery and makeup weren't really her thing. Her transformation could hardly have gone unnoticed in a village like the one she lived in. People had grouched, gossiped and jeered, but then they'd also had the flooding from the Dheune in winter, the August nights when it never got cooler than twenty degrees, and their respective health worries. Over time, seeing her at the market had become just as familiar a sight as the slightly sombre pediment on the church and the Christmas tinsel on the main street that still hadn't been taken down. To no longer see her would have garnered more attention.

When Nolwenn, who was never as shy as she seemed, commented that it couldn't have been easy at work *with all the kids*, Claudie said that in fact teenagers generally respected her, that they had a certain level of open-mindedness, and that the people who reacted the worst were (here she started to count them on her bony fingers) drunk homeless people, groups of young men, and poor women, who were often pushing prams. One of these women had once chased her in the supermarket; Claudie had had to hide behind the fish counter, from where she could hear her continuing to hurl abuse on the other side.

'Well, I'm certainly never as relaxed as I would be back at home in the sticks.' She looked at herself in the mirror, moving a few hairs across her forehead with her ring finger. 'And here,' she continued. 'Really – with all of you, I feel good . . . I feel like myself.'

Silver-grey is perfectly nice, perfectly chic, but Madame Lévy-Leroyer wants to try something else. She and Clara go through the various colours that might suit her sharp, bony face, which is redeemed by emerald-green eyes. Eventually she finds one. *Ah, I've got it! A Bernadette Chirac–style blonde.* Madame Habib, who is busy copying out names into a brand-new notebook, casts a concerned look over her glasses. She has just heard the name of her greatest rival.

Lorraine went to see Doctor Maître about her dizzy spells, and he suggested she have an MRI scan. She has an appointment at Creusot Hospital in twelve days' time. Maître didn't dare risk a diagnosis, but Lorraine is convinced she has a brain tumour. *I have been too unhappy, and it's finally caught up with me.* This morning she hasn't said a word. She arrived with two little packets of speculoos biscuits in addition to the usual coffees, sat down on her stool and has barely opened her mouth since. She cast a melancholic glance around the salon and looked at Nolwenn and then Clara, as if saying, *Well, ladies, it's been fun. I'll miss you all.*

After she left, Nolwenn took the two packets of speculoos from the counter while her first customer was paying. She slipped one into her pocket and opened the other to eat there and then.

He arrives in the middle of a Wednesday afternoon, without an appointment. It's autumn, and daylight is already fading. Nolwenn is on a management course and Madame Habib has gone out to buy paracetamol. It hasn't been a busy day.

Clara can tell instantly that he isn't from the area. From the way he holds himself, the way he asks *Is it OK if I don't have an appointment?* His movements are loose and nervous. He quickly sinks into the chair and immediately stops moving. She tells herself he must be an artist or an actor – yes, an actor; there are plenty of actors who aren't well known. She doesn't dare place her hands on his shoulders.

'What are we thinking today?'

'Ah, um, something clean-cut. Short. Well, the important thing is that it's clean-cut. I trust you.'

'How do you normally style it, sir?'

He passes a hand over his head, from right to left. 'Like this.'

'And we'll get rid of the hair at the back of the neck?'

'Yes.'

'Straight or slightly faded?'

'Straight is perfect.'

His hair is very fine; she runs her fingers through it and it's like silk. Even the slightest snip will be noticeable, so she'll have to pay attention, take her time.

'There's a lump there from when I was born; don't be alarmed.'

'No problem.'

The shampoo. He closes his eyes, and she takes the opportunity to look at his face upside down, telling herself that he must be practising his lines. Why does she feel the need to imagine that he's an actor? She wonders if they would be happy together. Maybe – if she were an actor too. Or an artist. Not a hairdresser, at any rate. If they were together, would she still fancy him after three years of living together?

They do not speak while she's cutting his hair. You often dread silence in a salon; you feel like you have to fill it, but it doesn't happen this time. It is a focused silence, a comfortable silence, not one of absence or emptiness. 'Tout doucement' by Bibie is playing on Radio Nostalgie. Clara thinks it's a wonderful song and promises herself that she'll listen to it again on the bus. This happens to her quite regularly. She is moved by a song she had forgotten about and plans to find it again on YouTube when she has a moment. But when she leaves the salon, she gets caught up in all sorts of other things – buying milk, calling her mother – and she never does.

The man opens his eyes and smiles at her. She does the same, then lowers her gaze. She'd still fancy this one, even after three years.

And then Madame Habib arrives and 'Tout doucement' gives way to an advert for E. Leclerc supermarkets. Jacqueline wipes her feet on the doormat.

'The cross on the pharmacy is falling off; it's hanging by a thread. It's quite remarkable.'

She realises she doesn't recognise the person whose hair Clara is doing – and it's a man, no less. There is an immediate shift: she goes into *Man at the salon* mode. Standing up very straight, she hangs her coat on the rail and caresses the backs of the chairs as she passes, as if expressing some kind of irrepressible sensuality. It does not suit her.

When Clara has finished, the man gets up and they become strangers once again. At the same moment, Madame Chicheportiche arrives with her grandson, Ferdinand. It's Wednesday; she has picked him up from his trombone lesson and taken him *to the hairdressers*. Clara takes their coats and goes to hang them on the rail. When she gets back, the man has gone. He hasn't left a tip. She is a little disappointed – not about the tip, but because she won't see him again. She sits Ferdinand down, and, as she's stepping on the pedal to raise the seat, her gaze is drawn to an object on the little table. A book, left behind by the man. A paperback. She won't go out to catch up with him – it'll be a good reason for him to come back to the salon. Then she realises that if Madame Habib spots it, she'll be more than happy to chase after him to return it. She edges closer to the little table, opens the drawer and pops the book inside, just as naturally as if it were a comb or a pair of scissors. Jacqueline hasn't seen; she is listening to Madame Chicheportiche talking about a little house she has just inherited. *With wisteria above the door, just like I've always wanted.*

Clara feels better. With the book in the drawer, it's as if the man is still there. She runs her hand through Ferdinand's hair and then places it on his shoulder. Ferdinand is changing; he's getting broader and more confident. Well, in the way he looks. When he answers her questions, his cheeks still glow red as ever.

It is only later, when she opens the drawer to get a scrunchie, that she rediscovers the book she'd since forgotten about. She thinks about the man again, about his air of mystery, his graceful nervousness. He hasn't come back to the salon. What if he left the book behind on purpose? She looks at the title and the cover. There's a woman in a beautiful chiffon dress and a little boy with pink cheeks. A detail from an old painting. Clara opens it and flicks through it, spotting a page with the corner folded down towards the end of the first third. A sentence has been underlined in blue ballpoint pen. *You have a soul in you of rare quality, an artist's nature; never let it starve for lack of what it needs.*

She slips the book into her bag. It will remain there until the following Monday when she is tidying her shopping bag and places the book on the living room table at home before getting distracted by a visit from a neighbour. The next morning, it will catch the eye of JB, who wanders into the room with his bowl of Chocapic and picks it up in passing, glances at the title, the author's name and the detail from the painting on the cover, feels nothing special and leaves it at one end of the coffee table, a little further from where he found it. A few days later, the cat knocks it off as he awkwardly lands from a jump from the sofa, a fall that has him running out of the room as if he'd just seen a madman with a gun. That same evening, Clara will pick the book up and put it in the bookcase in the corridor, on the same shelf as *L'Appel de l'ange* and *La Fille de papier* by Guillaume Musso, *Ma médecine naturelle* by Dr Fabrice Visson, *Glacé* by Bernard Minier, *I Am Zlatan Ibrahimović* by Zlatan Ibrahimović, *The Secret* by Rhonda Byrne (a gift from Anaïs, Clara's childhood friend), *The 30 Most Beautiful Hiking Routes in Burgundy* (a gift from her father), *Trois baisers* by Katherine Pancol, *Bélier: Daily Horoscopes*, the 2011,

2013, 2015, 2016 and 2018 editions, as well as a dozen Akira Toriyama mangas, which JB loves. The book will stay there for precisely five months, twenty-nine days, two hours and forty-seven minutes.

It is the middle of the afternoon on a Sunday in March. She has just woken up from a nap. The snow is no longer falling but its brightness is still being projected onto the ceiling of their apartment. It is rather lovely. The cat is watching her from a pouffe opposite the sofa with a look that says, *Who are you and what are you doing in my house?*, before opening his mouth in an enormous yawn. JB has been helping a friend move house since the morning, and lunch at her parents' has been cancelled.

She takes advantage of how quiet the apartment is and has a bath, then she calls her mother. Afterwards, she gets a chicken and mushroom pie out of the freezer for dinner and makes herself a cup of tea. While the water is boiling, she receives a message from JB (*We're going back to Sevrey, we won't be done until the evening*) and she sends back two emojis (flexed biceps and a kiss). She opens Instagram, closes it again very quickly, puts her phone down on the counter and looks out of the window, thinking that she could quite happily make love in this moment. The snow, the cold and the soft silence probably have something to do with it. She could happily make love to Jacob Elordi. She discovered him for the first time this week in a series she was watching with JB. Every time he appeared on screen, she wondered if she was managing to hide her attraction to him. She has always liked tall, slim, borderline skinny men. Like the customer who came into the salon a little while ago. She hasn't forgotten his long hands and slender fingers, imagining them clasped around her waist. She also remembers his mouth, picturing it slightly open, breathing warm air, just a few centimetres from her own. She doesn't know why this image has such an effect on her . . .

He left a book at the salon. A paperback. What was it again?

II

MARCEL

Nothing at first. *Nada, niente, nichts.* There's that first sentence, as famous as an advertising slogan or the chorus of a song from childhood, and then it all gets complicated. The words are like lines of ants before her eyes. It's about François I, Charles V and metempsychosis. François I is a king of France. Charles V's story is already more complex. And it's not like she'd have heard of metempsychosis at the salon or from JB. What *is* this book?

She has a sip of tea, pulls the tartan blanket back over her legs and carries on reading. One sentence stands out to her like somebody waving. *I would lay my cheeks gently against the comfortable cheeks of my pillow, as plump and blooming as the cheeks of babyhood.* She is moved by this image, and even more moved by what follows. It is about a moment of mistaken joy. A man wakes up in bed. He is in pain and is glad to see light underneath the door. It is morning and he can ask for help. But no: the ray of light comes from a gas lamp that has just been extinguished in the corridor. It is still nighttime; he has only been asleep for a few minutes and will have to endure several more hours yet . . .

She carries on reading, wanting to know more – she is curious and always has been. Another sentence stops her in her tracks: *When a man is asleep, he has in a circle round him the chain of the hours, the sequence of the years, the order of the heavenly host.* Impenetrable. She frowns but continues, no longer quite so moved. The words become lines of ants once more. Proust is talking about the position of his body in the bed, about his stiff arm and the furniture situated around him. So many words, simply to say that he can't sleep – the guy obviously has a problem; he should get some help.

She closes the book and chucks it onto the sofa. That will do, thank you. There are plenty of people who like reading that kind of thing; she prefers Jacob Elordi. She turns to face the window, thinking about the actor's eyes and his sad cocker-spaniel expression, and then, strangely, as if something had just clicked in her brain, she remembers the last sentence she read. She picks the book up again and finds the page and sentence she is thinking of: *everything would be moving round me through the darkness: things, places, years.* And it suddenly makes sense. It's about a man in bed, drifting between sleep and wakefulness, dream and reality, past and present. His state of confusion is familiar to her. She too has experienced it when falling asleep or just after waking up, no longer sure if she's in her apartment, the house where she grew up or her grandmother's house in Besançon.

She sits up, concentrates. Proust hints that he's reaching the end of the back-and-forthing. At least, the character in his book does. At the close of one chapter, he says he is going to reflect on his life of old. To return to the past for good, and, just like Alice falling down the hole that took her to Wonderland, never come back. *In Search of Lost Time*. Why not go on the journey? She has always been interested in the past. The veils, the long dresses and the horse-drawn carriages dashing along cobbled roads. There used to be a print above the sofa in the living room of her nanny's house, of a painting which was probably from the same era as the book. It showed a woman standing in the wind. She had a long white skirt and was holding a green parasol to protect her from the sun. Clara had looked at it so intently that the woman appeared to be moving, and sometimes even turning around to silently watch her, her eyes narrowed in the blur of the distance. It's funny, it's been years since she's thought about it. And reading has brought this memory to mind, as if it had been hidden behind a folding screen that Proust has just moved with great delicacy.

She has only read about twelve pages, but she already knows how their relationship is going to play out. She will have to work hard and persevere with him, often through fog, sometimes in darkness, not be put off by his use of nested sentences and the imperfect subjective, exercising patience and a dictionary when necessary. And he, upon regular intervals, will blow her away just when she is least expecting it.

The more she reads, the better she understands him. He doesn't use complicated words – it's just that his sentences often *wander elsewhere*. Once she realises this, once she understands that he isn't abandoning her and will come back to find her, it all gets much easier. In fact, his sensitivity is what makes him so unique. People aren't used to *feeling* things so intensely in day-to-day life. And adapting to that level of subtlety is what requires effort on the part of the reader. That is what demands your full attention – and means you can't read *Swann's Way* with Rage Against the Machine playing in the background. Well, that's just an example.

Plus, why not admit it? She is rather proud: she is reading *In Search of Lost Time*. She can do it, and that is quite something.

Anaïs wouldn't be able to read *In Search of Lost Time*; Nolwenn doesn't even bear thinking about. And the fact that it started the way it did, by chance and out of sheer curiosity, adds to her growing sense of triumph.

'Are we eating?' JB is standing in front of her. The cat is staring at her with the same questioning look – he too must be hungry. 'It's nine fifteen. Aren't you hungry?'

'Yes, yes . . .' Clara stretches. 'I got a pie out of the freezer; it just needs heating up.'

'I'll do it if you want.'

'No, I'll make a salad to go with it.' She gets up. 'I have to stop at some point.'

She tends to the pie and the salad in the kitchen, then slips into the chair opposite JB, who starts telling her about Florian's move in minute detail.

'. . . the Kangoo was this far from the wall, no joke; my hand couldn't even fit between the two of them . . .'

She can see the words coming out of his mouth as he chews, she can see him picking the crumbs off his plate with his index finger, she can see the two scratches on his forearm, but her mind is far away, in a village named Combray at the end of the nineteenth century. There, in the child's bedroom of a timbered house, a poignant tragedy is playing out. Marcel, who clearly has sleeping problems, waits for just one thing when he goes to bed: his mother coming up to give him a kiss. On the evening in question, an impromptu visit from Swann, a family friend, delays even further his mother's kiss. Marcel doesn't believe he can wait any longer, so he has an idea: he will write his mother a note, telling her he needs to see her as soon as possible, and give it to Françoise, the maid. She has just gone, missive in hand, and he is restlessly waiting for his mother to arrive . . .

'Aren't you going to finish that?' JB gestures towards the remains of the pie on her plate.

'Um . . . no.'

She is never very hungry in the evening. She slides the plate over to him. He devours its contents as though he hasn't eaten in three days.

'Are you OK?'

'Yes.'

'What did you do today?'

Today she started reading a book that was written over a hundred years ago by a man who never left his bed, a book with interminable sentences and which she feels, for a reason she still cannot understand, will make her stronger.

It's almost one a.m. by the time she stops reading. JB is asleep next to her. Their bodies do not touch, but she can feel the warmth of his skin.

Mamma Proust didn't respond well to her son's note. It went as badly as it could have done. *There is no answer*, is what she told Françoise. Marcel was distraught but, later, things started to go his way once more. After Swann left, he heard his mother on the stairs and went out to see her. His father also came upstairs, and they all met in the corridor. When he saw his son in such a state, Papa Proust unexpectedly suggested that his wife spend the night with their child.

It doesn't fit in the tray, JB murmurs in his sleep, before rolling over and ending up on his back. Clara considers his half-open mouth and how it makes him look, then she turns to face the opposite direction, exhausted but with her eyes still open.

Marcel should have been happy that his mother was spending the night in his room, but he wasn't. Instead, he was now feeling her pain, the sadness that seeing her son cry had caused and the demeaning concession that this sadness had forced her to make.

This evidence of maternal weakness overshadowed any happiness he might have taken from having her there, any sense of personal victory.

She clasps her hands under her chin, closes her eyes and is instantly transported to the bedroom in Combray. From the window she watches Proust's parents seeing out Monsieur Swann, then she hears them talking about lobster, and coffee and pistachio ice cream. When she can no longer see them, she rushes out into the corridor, and Marcel's mother immediately appears, candle in hand.

She missed her bus stop. It's the first time it's happened. She got off at De-Lattre-de-Tassigny instead of Libération. The bus going back in the opposite direction wasn't for another thirteen minutes, so she walked to the salon and got there late.

All night she'd dreamed about a bell suspended from a garden gate, about the rustle of a chiffon dress in a staircase, about church bells ringing out in the evening silence. She'd been walking through a village as the sun went down, in her hand a note that vanished into thin air when it came to delivering it . . . On the bus she started reading again, not anticipating that she would read a passage so captivating that she wouldn't hear the voice announcement, with its tone slightly more quizzical the first time than the second: *Libération . . . Libération.*

The adult Marcel is drinking a mouthful of lime-flower tea, into which he has just dipped a madeleine. Something extraordinary starts to rise within him, taking on new life. *All the flowers in our garden and in M. Swann's park, and the water-lilies on the Vivonne and the good folk of the village and their little dwellings and the parish church and the whole of Combray and of its surroundings, taking their proper shapes and growing solid, sprang into being, town and gardens alike, from my cup of tea.* The passage is so powerful that she reads it again to experience the feeling once more, just like Marcel having another sip of tea to refresh the sensation of remembering.

It is so accurate, so true. She'd had her own madeleine moment several years ago, during a biology class at school. The good weather had returned, and someone was mowing the lawn outside the open windows. The sound of the engine's motor, coupled with the smell of freshly cut grass, had made her feel extraordinarily calm, as if somebody was there stroking her head. And there was more to it. The rumbling noise and the scent had had such an effect because they reminded her of a happy time in her past. A time at the house of her nanny, to be precise, who would often give the children she was looking after an afternoon snack of toasted baguette and a bar of milk chocolate. It was while she was sitting with the others at Madame Le Hennec's kitchen table for one of those snacks that Clara had heard the lawnmower outside and smelled the cut grass for the first time.

She'd been reminded of those childhood memories during that biology class. Of snack time, a sort of pause in an afternoon of games and hustle and bustle, the combination of milk chocolate and baguette so perfect that it felt they were designed to be eaten together. On the bus, the sensations she'd felt during the biology class came back to her. The first hot days of the year and the diffuse, unrestrained, almost painful sensuousness that came with them, the enjoyment of an easy lesson taught by a nice teacher, the names of the other students – Estelle Joffre, Nathan Girardin . . . The feeling of happiness the third time around was so strong that she considered turning to the people sitting near her and saying: *It's crazy, this thing about the madeleine that brings back the past; have you experienced that before too?* And that's when she heard the voice announcement: *De-Lattre-de-Tassigny . . . De-Lattre-de-Tassigny.*

'Had his mother put something in the tea?' says Madame Lopez, staring at her in the mirror.

'No, she didn't need to. The mere taste of the tea he is drinking at her house makes him remember the tea he drank at his aunt's when he was younger.'

Madame Habib peers over her glasses in their direction, wondering what they could possibly be talking about. Madame Lopez has given up trying to understand what Clara is saying and is staring at her own reflection, looking as if she's thinking, *I don't give a damn whether the guy had tea at his aunt's, his mother's or with the Queen of England, all I want is a good haircut.*

But Clara goes on. 'He wants to remain in the memory, so he drinks more tea, but it has less and less of an effect. A bit like waking up from a dream. The more you try to remember it, the less you're able to. Have you noticed that?'

Madame Lopez turns her head to the side, looks at her profile in the mirror, and replies: 'Woah, not too short.'

The poplar tree *praying for mercy, bowing in desperation before the storm* is magnificent. The final peals of thunder *growling among our lilac-trees* are magnificent. Marcel kissing the wind because it is the same air that his love has breathed, several miles away, is magnificent. As is *the orange light which glowed from the resounding syllable 'antes'* in the name 'Guermantes'; the moon *without display, suggesting an actress who does not have to come on for a while*; and reading, *a magic as potent as the deepest slumber.* Each time, she underlines the sentence or draws a little heart in the margin just next to it.

JB spent three quarters of an hour flicking through the photos on his phone before putting it down on his bedside table and nuzzling up against Clara. She can tell he is about to say something, which is annoying because she is reading a particularly absorbing part about the tumultuous relationship between Swann and Odette, about the one's jealousy and the other's lies. The book demands so much engagement; it establishes such a strong, all-encompassing relationship with the reader that it might seem to them that the people around them are conspiring to ruin their enjoyment. At least, that's how it feels to Clara, who has a growing desire to spend ten days all alone in the countryside, doing nothing but reading Proust.

JB looks at the book for a moment, his head resting on her shoulder, and then says, 'You love it, don't you? You're always reading it.'

She stops reading, momentarily giving up on finding out how Odette will respond to Swann, who has just asked if the rumours about her sleeping with women are true.

'I really like it.'

'Do you think I'd like it?'

'Mm, I don't think so, but who knows.'

'What's it about?'

She is tempted to say *Everything* but thinks that might be a little too vague.

'It's difficult to sum up.'

'Go on,' he says, placing a hand on her stomach underneath the blanket. 'I'm interested.'

She folds down the corner of page 409 and closes the book.

'So, at the beginning, Marcel – well, the hero of the book – is in bed, and he can't sleep, and he starts thinking about his past. First, his childhood, when he would go to his great-aunt's house in Combray. Well, she's horrible; she spends her days in bed looking out of the window, but he doesn't care, he mostly just goes for walks. So, he talks about everything he sees during his walks, the flowers, the landscapes, and he describes them in a super detailed way. At first, it's really strange but you quickly realise that he's giving you all this detail because he feels everything, he sees everything. He's a genius, basically. He talks about the people around him too. There's Swann, a guy who visits them. And Françoise, the maid. Her, I adore. She's direct, but she also mixes up her words. She's a really good cook, she makes a beef in aspic that makes you really want to find her recipe . . . Anyway, it starts like that, in the countryside, and then there's a change of scenery and we're in Paris, in a salon. Not a hairdressing salon, though. At the time, a salon was just people coming together to listen to music or do nothing really, just talk, talk about other people, gossip about them usually. The salon he's talking about is Madame Verdurin's. They call her the 'Patron' but she's ridiculous, just like all the people who go to her house. Like, when she laughs, she doesn't want to open her mouth because she's dislocated her jaw, so she hunches over and buries her head in her hands. There's also a guy, I can't remember his name, but when he hears someone talking about the colour *blanche* he yells *Blanche of Castile!* just like that, thinking it makes him sound intelligent even though he isn't at all; it has nothing to do with that so it's just stupid. And then . . . Where was I? . . . Ah yes, we meet Swann again at Verdurin's. But he shouldn't really be there, he is above everyone who's there – he has class, you know. In fact, he goes there just to be with Odette, who he's obsessed with. He wants to know what she does when he isn't with her; he searches for her in all the local restaurants and looks through her window. And the thing that's really weird is that the first time he saw her he didn't even like her. He thought she was ugly and could tell she was hiding things from him. And she also uses English words when she talks, like *lunch* instead of *déjeuner* – it's super irritating. And actually, he only becomes obsessed with her because she eludes him. That says something pretty significant about us, when you think about it. It says that love isn't something that just happens to us – we decide to love. And we decide to love what we don't have, simply because we don't have it.'

She pauses, realising that she's probably said enough for such a late hour. JB doesn't respond. She looks down and sees that his eyes are closed, and his chest is rising and falling. He is asleep, of course. He must have given up when she started talking about the detail and precision of the Proustian descriptions.

The idea just came to her one day. She'd closed the book after
finishing a chapter and looked at the young women lying on the
grass in white dresses on the cover, which she had never taken the
time to do before. She liked how the book looked on the mustard-
yellow mohair blanket covering her legs (she was on the balcony
at her sister's in Louhans), so she took a photo and posted it on
Instagram, adding the Juno filter and the hashtags *MarcelProust*,
InSearchOfLostTime, *WithinABuddingGrove*, *Bookstagram* and
Bookish.

She went back on Instagram at around ten o'clock that night.
The photo had ten likes. In comparison, her most liked post, a
photo of a cat nestled in JB's sports bag with only its head poking
out, had 193.

Madame Bozonnet comes into the salon to cancel her afternoon appointment. She fainted in the shopping arcade at Carrefour and the paramedics took her to hospital, where she is waiting to be examined . . . That doesn't make sense. Clara turns around to look at the till. It is not Madame Bozonnet but in fact her husband, who has come in to cancel his wife's appointment. They have exactly the same weak, hesitant, *apologetic* voice.

Lorraine shows up at the salon, triumphant. The MRI scan showed she doesn't have a brain tumour. Doctor Maître told her she was probably suffering from *something something* anxiety and recommended she see a psychoanalyst to try and find out why. And so she's looking for a shrink, which, in this area, is proving a challenge. Especially since she wants someone who *accepts insurance reimbursement forms (I'm still paying off three loans!).* Never has a woman been so happy to discover that she has episodic paroxysmal anxiety.

The thing she likes most is the rhythm it imposes. You are forced to take your time while also paying attention – it is very unique like that. How many times while reading has her mind wandered from the words on the page to making a shopping list or thinking back to a conversation she had at the salon during the day? Time and attention, relaxation and concentration. Proust is her yoga.

To read it well, you must allow yourself to skip passages too. She sometimes skims through five pages and starts reading from the beginning of the next chapter. With over four thousand pages in the whole of *In Search of Lost Time*, there's a bit of wiggle room. She does this without any qualms, certain that if Marcel were reading it today, even he would find it too long at times.

Given the average age of the regulars at Cindy Coiffure, it is not a big surprise when one of them dies. When Madame Habib hears, she will sigh, then remove said customer's record from her little revolving stand, rip it into four pieces and deposit it in the recycling bin (she thinks throwing them in would be disrespectful). The news will spread through the salon and the atmosphere will get a little heavy for a few hours, then life will go back to normal. When it came to Madame Da Silva, who had been the salon's longest-standing customer, Jacqueline was determined to go to the funeral. She stopped by the salon on her way, and it was clear that she'd given it her all: a mantilla made of Calais lace, a black velvet dress decorated with a pendant of the Virgin, and black sunglasses *à la* Jackie O. She couldn't have been any more chic, not even if she were attending the funeral of a Portuguese infante.

Claudie Hansen arrives to the opening bars of 'Coup de soleil' by Richard Cocciante. She is greeted by Clara. Madame Habib was invited to a wedding and has taken the Saturday off. Patrick is in. Nolwenn, who is concentrating on straightening Madame Rinaldi's hair, doesn't even look up.

She is more relaxed than she was on her last visit, but she hasn't yet learned to make the best of herself. Her unstyled hair falls like rope on both sides of her face, making it look bigger. She is wearing makeup, but it lacks precision, her collarbones are sticking out, and her ballet flats emphasise the length of her feet. Looking at her, you might see someone who is exhausted from being torn between two personas. And yet, that smile . . .

After she has washed her hair, Clara asks Patrick for his opinion. He replies without interrupting Madame Castaneda's blow-dry: 'I'd do highlights and a soft fringe to hide the forehead a bit. Then a blow-dry, and if it's still too flat, why not try a bit of a perm, but not tight curls – something subtle, like what I did for Anne-Gaëlle last Saturday.'

It's more or less what Clara had in mind. She discusses it with

Claudie, who looks at her in the mirror, punctuating each of her sentences with an *OK . . . OK . . .* She is fine with anything. And there isn't any more to it, judging from her expression – what matters is that she's there. She settles into the chair, crosses her legs and stops moving. Roch Voisine has taken over from Richard Cocciante.

'Ah, I don't believe it!' she says, sitting up in her chair. 'Is it you who's reading that?'

She is talking about *Within a Budding Grove*, which Clara had left on the little table on her way back from lunch.

'That book saved my life!' says Claudie, picking it up.

Clara's face breaks into a childish smile. If she had eyes in the back of her head, she'd be able to see Nolwenn limply looking up, surprised by this unusual exchange.

Claudie turns the book over, looks at the back cover, and turns it over again.

'What a beauty! Where have you got to?'

'The beginning. When he's playing with Gilberte.'

'In the gardens of the Champs-Élysées.'

'That's it.' Clara seems to be hesitating, then she edges closer and whispers, 'Incidentally, at one point, I'm not sure I get it. He's playing hide and seek with Gilberte, he falls on top of her, and – how can I say it . . .'

'He orgasms! Exactly!'

The voices around them fall silent. Patrick sniggers. Even Roch Voisine seems to be singing more quietly.

Claudie waits for the noise to pick up again before saying, 'It's very organic, *In Search of Lost Time*. It says a lot about bodies, about skin. Proust describes clothing incredibly precisely so you can sense the bodies underneath it. Bodies shaped by desire. That's why his characters often have red faces.'

Clara doesn't move, taken in by the words that have just come out of the school bus driver's mouth. Claudie goes on: 'He's going to leave for Balbec, you'll see, it's a wonderful section . . . Is it the first one you've read, or have you read others?'

'I read *Swann's Way* first. What about you?'

'Oh, I've read the whole of *In Search of Lost Time,* several times! And I often reread parts of it. Proust really saved my life, I swear. I'll tell you about it one day.'

Slowly, as if the wave of this pleasant surprise is still moving through her, she puts the book back down where she found it. Then she sinks into the chair, studies Clara in the mirror and announces, 'I knew you weren't like the others.'

With Proust, she feels like she can see everything. She is bound to, since he shows her both the visible world in all its infinite detail and another one that's just behind it, out of sight but large and powerful, which imposes its own law and passion above all else: that of people's mental and psychological realities. And that's not all. In introducing her to the idea of involuntary memory, taking her by the shoulders and shifting her position just very slightly, he has expanded her mind by adding an element that she had not before considered: time. When the past emerges in the present, is it not a continuation of it? Isn't a memory more real than the time it comes from? Why do we seem to remember things better and better as we grow older?

What a gift. She is thinking about this one morning while she's listening to Nolwenn talk about *The Real Housewives of Beverly Hills* with a customer. Time spent reading Proust is time gained, time stolen away *by* intelligence rather than *from* it.

'Clara, I'd like to speak to you.'

'Everything alright, Jacqueline?'

'Yes, yes, it's just . . . it's Madame Lopez. She just called to make an appointment and she's asked for Nolwenn to do her hair.'

'Nolwenn? But I do Madame Lopez's hair.'

'That's why I wanted to talk to you. I don't think she was very happy last time.'

'I did the same as usual last time.'

'It's not about the hair. Last time I heard you telling her some story about a guy who drinks a tea that sends him back to his past.'

'Ah, yes, no, I told her the story of the madeleine moment from Proust. She didn't know it.'

'You're reading Proust?'

'Yes – well, I was reading *Swann's Way*. But now I'm on *Within a Budding Grove*.'

'But why?'

'*Why?*'

'Are you doing an exam?'

'No, it's just for pleasure. Have you read it?'

'Yes – well no, but near enough.'

'You should, I'm sure you'd like it.'

'Of course. But in the meantime, I think that's what Madame Lopez *didn't* like. I noticed that she looked uncomfortable. You shouldn't talk about it with customers; it'll make them feel insecure.'

'I talked about it with Claudie, and it didn't make her feel insecure. She even invited me to her house to talk about it.'

'Claudie?'

'Hansen. The school bus driver. She says Proust changed her life.'

'But you're not going there to do her hair?'

'No, don't worry. That's not why I'm going, and anyway, she loves coming here. We're just going to talk about Proust and drink tea.'

Raymonde's Story, Continued

I had a look in the shed when I knew he wasn't there, and it confirmed that he'd spent the night there. He'd found a blanket in the garage and slept underneath it. And in the evening, from the kitchen window, I saw him returning to it. I felt sorry that he was sleeping there, but then I'd see the Chinese woman hopping on one leg to get her knickers back on and it set me straight. He didn't try to talk to me either, figuring I wasn't interested, and time passed like that – me at home, him in the shed, not speaking. Sometimes I would see him leaving or coming back. If we caught each other's eye, we would immediately turn around again. At night I could hear him coming into the house. He would help himself to whatever was in the fridge, taking cheese, ham, like a little mouse. Or he would go looking for tools in the garage. About a month went by, I'd say, and then one day, he came to see me. Listen, Raymonde, I can't do this any more, I'm not a dog, you have to take me back. I'd been thinking about it a lot and had a response prepared. I'm happy for you to come back, but on one condition. That you let me do one thing first. He threw himself at my feet. Anything you want! he said, clutching my legs so tightly that I almost fell over . . . Oh, I didn't waste any time. The next morning it was nice weather, I remember; I left home at ten on the dot and headed towards Saint-Marcel. There I stopped outside Chez Blériot, the butcher's. Let me tell you, I was not over-confident. My heart was almost exploding, and my legs could barely support me. I glanced inside and saw that Bernard, the butcher, was on his own. There weren't any customers, and the apprentice wasn't in. I can't let this opportunity pass me by, I thought, and I went inside. Bernard greeted me: Ah, Raymonde, you're in luck, I've got tête de veau, you're going to love it. I didn't say much, and he asked me if everything was OK. Yes, I said, it's just I have something to ask you, which isn't easy to ask. Well, that's something else, he said, placing his hands far apart on the work surface. I'm listening. I looked him right in the eye and began: Bernard, d'you know how long we've known each other? He was so surprised by the question that he didn't react. Thirty-seven years, I said, just like that. When you've known someone for thirty-seven years, you trust them, right? He turned his head to the side without taking his eyes off me. Raymonde, I'm worried about you, what's going on? So I plucked up the courage and said it: What's going on is that I want to spend the night with you. Just one night. And afterwards I won't ask you for anything else, I promise.

Proust isn't difficult, it's just different.

But still, he could start a new paragraph a little more often.

In the meantime, she reads thirty pages every day, on the bus, on her lunch breaks and at bedtime. Proust is no Harlan Coben, and, considering the rhythm that reading it requires, this is quite an achievement, especially for a busy person.

'I think I'm going to have a lie-down.'

'Everything OK?' asks her mother.

'Is it something you ate?' says her father.

'I'm not feeling well,' she says, rubbing her stomach.

'You *are* looking a bit peaky.'

'Aren't you going to come for a walk?'

'No, Dad, I need to lie down.'

'That's a shame. It's actually sunny for once.'

'Don't put pressure on her, Yves. You know Clara's always had painful periods.'

'Mum . . .'

'There's no point beating around the bush.'

'But you were fine this morning,' says JB.

'It's just started.'

'D'you want to go home?'

'No, it's fine, I'll go and lie down. Then you can all still enjoy yourselves.'

When she gets to her room, she realises she's forgotten a vital detail. She goes back down to the living room, where her mother is telling a story she's already heard a hundred times about an old work colleague whose periods were so painful that she would pinch her arms until they bruised to take her mind off the pain. Clara grabs her bag, pulling a face like someone who's lost their mind. Once she's back in her room she straightens her pillows, sits in bed and picks up her bag, from which she removes *Within a Budding Grove*. And then she lets out a long sigh of contentment.

She had her period ten days ago. She just couldn't bear to listen to her parents and JB discussing the relative benefits of savings accounts and life insurance any longer, much less accompanying them on the ambling walk that would follow, especially when the Baron de Charlus had just appeared in *In Search of Lost Time*, with all the discretion of a huge fly landing upon a ball of mozzarella.

It is something she has noticed before. She gets her best, most lucid and most constructive ideas during the final stretch of the bus journey, after the old bridge – probably because she knows she only has a few more minutes of freedom.

This morning is no different. Just as the bus reaches the other side of the Saône, she looks up from her book and has a realisation. She has always had a feel for words, for their precision and musicality – the thing that characterises her passion for this book and its author. Like land left fallow, it simply hadn't had a focus until she came to open this particular book.

Well, maybe that wasn't quite right. Thinking about it further, it happened to be this book, but she could just have easily become obsessed with chess, or with cultivating bonsai trees or making perfume. What was already within her was room for a passion that was challenging and all-encompassing. And intelligent.

The beginning of *The Guermantes Way*, which is about the Proust family moving into an apartment within the Guermantes residence, is a shock that she had not anticipated. She never wants to leave the apartment again, especially Françoise's kitchen; she fears that the story will take her somewhere else. As she reads these pages, something verging on magical happens, making her think for the very first time that books might be better than real life.

'I didn't fit in anywhere. Everyone fits in somewhere; I tried but it didn't work – I felt like a cat who'd been asked to solve an equation with two unknowns. I started to hate myself, and I was exhausted too. Not being able to be yourself is exhausting. I wrote a letter explaining everything, I took a pack of sleeping pills washed down with Cointreau, lay on my bed and went to sleep. But I'd spoken to my mother in the morning, and she knew something was up. She got the firefighters to break down the door since she lived 600 kilometres away, and I woke up in hospital, very unhappy that I was still alive. An ex came to visit me. We weren't together but we still saw each other. She was a second-hand bookseller in Yonne, near Colette's house, and she'd been nagging me to read Proust for years. This time she'd brought a copy of *Swann's Way*. I remember that on the cover there was a rather ugly watercolour of a young boy's face, a cup of tea and some madeleines. One morning I opened it, on a beautiful autumn morning in the hospital gardens, and it dazzled me. Every part of it spoke to me, straight away. Its sensitivity, its sense of beauty. This guy who was forced to withdraw from life because of his frailty, who devoted entire pages to falling asleep or describing a hawthorn bush. He was as lost in the world as I was. I was no longer alone. I was saved.'

Claudie's house is like her. Made of wood and single storey, it feels as though it wasn't completed in one go but has been put together over time and slightly randomly, with objects in places you wouldn't expect (she will later reveal that she made a good deal of them herself). Large rooms that are pleasant to walk around and to be in, with plenty of sofas, armchairs and cushions. And cats too, who, unlike others cats, allow you to stroke them, and even respond when spoken to. It smells of orange and cedar, and yellow net curtains hang from the windows: they could easily be in a canyon on the outskirts of Los Angeles in the early seventies.

Sitting between two large cushions covered in a paisley print fabric, legs tucked underneath her, is Claudie, radiant in a big diamond-print jumper that looks like a minidress on her. Clara has realised that for Claudie it isn't about the way clothes make her look. Simply being a woman seems to be enough for her to be happy. A small dog of indeterminate breed who has a problem with one eye is nuzzled up against her. He stares into the void ahead of him, head resting on his front paws, waiting for sleep to take hold.

'The more you read, the more you like it, have you noticed?'

'You do,' says Clara. 'Because you get used to its rhythm. At the start you're like *I don't understand, this sentence should end and yet it's carrying on*, but that's because you're reading it too quickly. That's a mistake. You have to take your time, take breaks. Now, when I read it, I feel like I can hear it speaking to me.'

'A true Proustian . . . And the humour – have you noticed how funny it is?'

'Yes! It's very visual; it's a lot like being in a film at times. Like when he gets out of the carriage because he's spotted a girl on the pavement, then he bumps into Madame Verdurin and she thinks he's come running out because of her.'

'It's wonderful! And it gets funnier and funnier – you'll see. Have you started *The Guermantes Way*?'

'Yes, I read the beginning and loved it, but I stopped to reread *Swann in Love*. I'm not sure why.'

'That happens with this book. You often feel the need to retrace your steps – probably to make sure you haven't missed anything. Anyway, you're going to enjoy *Guermantes*. It's full of very funny salon scenes.'

The little dog yaps and lifts his head as if he's responding to this last comment, then leaps from the sofa and runs off. Clara turns around and sees him enthusiastically greeting a woman who has just entered the room. She's in her sixties, with round glasses and dishevelled salt-and-pepper hair.

'Clara, this is Michèle,' says Claudie, stretching out her legs. 'My wife. I don't think you've met.'

So Claudie still had a wife. Clara had heard about her, but put the information to one side, assuming the couple had broken up when Claudie came into being.

'You are so pretty,' says Michèle, touching her head. 'So, you're the hairdresser who's reading Marcel Proust? You'll have to tell me how you're doing it. I've never been able to. It sends me straight to sleep!'

'She thinks he's just a high-society author,' says Claudie. 'I've told her so many times that he isn't . . .'

'What bothers me is that he stayed nice and cosy in his bed telling stories about duchesses, while an entire generation was being wiped out in the trenches.'

'He was asthmatic, he could hardly even drag himself out of bed and down the stairs of his own home! And I'm not talking about his hypersensitivity. Come on, Michèle, the sound of a spoon clinking against a glass could make him faint, how did you expect him to go to war? Instead, he did humanity a favour by writing an international literary masterpiece.'

Clara watches them, looking at one and then the other, like at a game of tennis.

'He could have at least talked about it,' says Michèle.

'About what?'

'The war. And the living conditions of the working class at the time, of the children who were sent into factories.'

'He talks about the war! That's all he talks about in *Time Regained*. As for the living conditions of the working class, you've got Zola or Louise Michel, who do that very well. But even if Proust had been poor, I don't think he'd have written that different a book. I think he would have noticed the same pettiness, the same hypocrisy.'

'She has an answer for everything,' Michèle says to Clara, placing a hand on her shoulder. 'You're staying for dinner.'

'Umm . . .'

'Oh, I'm not giving you a choice. I have tomatoes and feta from the market, I'm going to make a Greek salad. And you can try the bread we make; you can tell me what you think.'

Her gaze falls briefly on her wife, and, seemingly reassured that everything in the living room is as it should be, just like it is in her life, she leaves, with the half-blind dog trailing after her.

Clara turns to Claudie, who is extracting herself from the sofa.

'I'm going to show you something. Come.'

She takes her into the next room, a sort of antechamber with nothing but a women's bike in it, then into another one, a small library with a low ceiling and walls of shelves that are bowing under the weight of books, old LPs and rows of CDs. It is the latter she is interested in.

'You said you're now rereading...?

'*Swann in Love.*'

'*Swann in Love*,' echoes Claudie, removing the corresponding case from the collection.

She says nothing more and leads Clara back through the living room. They exit the room via a small glass door and sit down underneath a porch at the back of the house. It looks out on a landscape that slopes down, then up again, before finally disappearing into a haze in which only a few tiled roofs huddled around a church are visible. Claudie abandons her guest for a few minutes, returning with two bottles of Heineken and a CD player in the shape of a large stone. She offers Clara a beer, lights herself a cigarette and slides the CD into the slot. Then she sinks into a wicker chair, rests her feet on the ledge in front of her and waits, looking out at the countryside.

And there, in a remote corner of Saône-et-Loire, with the sky turning pink and the song of a particularly loquacious blackbird in the background, the voice of André Dusollier begins to fill the air – the lovely, warm, friendly voice of André Dussollier. *Dr Cottard was never quite certain of the tone in which he ought to reply to any observation, or whether the speaker was jesting or in earnest . . .*

In the bath, she comes across a phrase that she has to read five times before she understands it:

That was enough to reawaken in him the old anguish, that lamentable and inconsistent excrescence of his love, which held Swann ever at a distance from what she really was, like a yearning to attain the impossible (what this young woman really felt for him, the hidden longing that absorbed her days, the secret places of her heart), for between Swann and her whom he loved this anguish piled up an unyielding mass of already existing suspicions, having their cause in Odette, or in some other perhaps who had preceded Odette, allowing this now ageing lover to know his mistress of the moment only in the traditional and collective phantasm of the 'woman who made him jealous', in which he had arbitrarily incarnated his new love.

Meaning Swann feels unjustifiably jealous of his new conquest because he has been jealous of other women before her, and of Odette in particular.

Once she understands this, it becomes perfectly clear. It even occurs to her that it would be impossible to say it as well, or as *accurately*, in any other way.

It began with the thought that Nolwenn's mannerisms were similar to those of Françoise from *In Search of Lost Time*. Then it was Madame Habib who seemed like a character from the book, with her fits of snobbery, her physical and verbal tics, and her mournful, frog-like eyes. Clara eventually realised that the book is so vast and encompasses so many topics that it is virtually impossible not to see the world through its lens while you are reading it. Even the smallest things become Proustian. A cluster of wisteria, the violet colour of its flowers against its green leaves. Dust suspended in a shaft of light in an otherwise dark room. And Annick, her mother, who always turns her head slightly and half opens her mouth when she is photographed, as if there is someone calling her at the exact same moment. That is Proustian, truly Proustian.

She reads Proust before she goes to bed, and often she sees flowers when she closes her eyes. Nasturtiums in bright sunshine, hedges of almond-scented flowering hawthorne, apple trees in blossom swaying in spring rain. And lilacs like the ones on the way to Swann's park, bouquets of violets like the ones in Odette's corsage, Pennsylvania roses like the ones in Balbec, forget-me-nots, poppies and periwinkles. Their colours stick in her mind and seep into her dreams, which, also being subject to Proustian influence, have never been as creative nor as prodigious.

Now, when reading, she records her thoughts in a little pink notebook, just like Claudie suggested:

People spend their time watching others in this book. Swann watches Odette, Marcel watches Gilberte, Marcel watches the Duchesse de Guermantes.

Name 'Guermantes' is like a balloon that bursts and then the whole of Combray appears.

We don't do things for the reasons we think we do.

She also jotted down the sentences that have made an impression on her, for one reason or another:

A moist and gentle breeze was blowing.

He realised, too, that Odette's qualities were not such as to justify his setting so high a value on the hours he spent in her company.

An event for which we are longing never happens quite in the way we have been expecting, failing the advantages on which we supposed that we might count, others present themselves for which we never hoped, and make up for our disappointment.

We are not provided with wisdom, we must discover it for ourselves, after a journey through the wilderness which no one else can take for us, an effort which no one can spare us, for our wisdom is the point of view from which we come at last to regard the world.

Existence to us is hardly interesting save on the days on which the dust of realities is shot with magic sand.

. . . on which the dust of realities is shot with magic sand.

Proust. Until now, that mythical name had meant as much to her as one of those towns – Capri, St Petersburg . . . – in which she knew she would never set foot.

He has never been good with words, especially when it comes to important things. She knows this, so he must have prepared, perhaps even practised his lines by himself in the Dacia Duster or outside the building before coming up – she can sense it from his manner, from the look in his eyes, from the way he is speaking. Nothing about any of it is normal. And despite all this, he still doesn't manage to soften the blow of what he has to say, not least because he has chosen a bad time to do it. It's a radiant Easter Monday after twenty days of rain. Clara only has one thing in mind, and that's getting through the rest of the ironing so she can dash over to her sister's wonderful balcony and read more of *The Guermantes Way*.

And then he announces: 'Clara, I've got something not very nice to tell you. Basically, I've met someone, and I'd like to see how it goes with her.'

He glances down at his jeans pocket, now emitting the unbearable opening bars of 'The Final Countdown', which he recently set as his ringtone after hearing it on an episode of *Monster Jam*. There's a palpable sense of hesitation – he seems unsure about whether to take the call or not.

'Do you want to . . .?' asks Clara.

'No, they can leave a message.'

'No, I mean . . . Do you want to break up?'

'Ah. Yes, actually.'

It's a disaster: they can't really hear one another, can't understand each other, just as deep down, they've never really heard or understood one another. He waits until it's silent again, and then says, 'I will always love you, that won't change. I just want to move forward with someone else.'

It's exactly the kind of sentence that he'd have had to practise saying; perhaps it had even been suggested by the person he wants to move forward with (*Tell her you'll always love her, it'll take the edge off*).

Clara folds her arms across her chest, then lifts one hand and places it on her neck. JB asks if she's OK.

'Yes, I'm just . . . I'm just surprised.'

'We don't have sex any more.'

She knew he would mention that.

'I counted,' he adds. 'It's been ten months. Ten months, do you realise that?'

'I know.'

'I'm twenty-five and you're twenty-three.'

'I know.'

It's a bit like she's watching a rocket at lift-off. Something is clearly happening; there are rumbling sounds and fire, but it doesn't move; it remains intact, feeling nothing, perhaps, but a little bit of heat. She doesn't want to cry or hurl the first thing she can find at JB's face; she doesn't even feel the need to sit down. It occurs to her that he could have waited until evening to talk to her (she'll never be able to read *The Guermantes Way* now), and then she looks up at him and asks, 'Who is she?', in the curious but rational tone of someone asking a waiter what's in the potato salad.

He has no intention of disclosing this information, and, being of a naturally gentle disposition, indicates this by softly closing his eyes.

'You can tell me,' Clara insists. 'I won't try to contact her. You know me, I'm not like that. I just don't want to look stupid if she turns up at the salon.'

'No, she doesn't go to the salon. She goes to one in Beaune.'

'Is she from Beaune?'

JB grants her a nod.

'That's where you went to talk about your job. So she's a teacher over there and you met when you went into her class? Just tell me if I'm right; I won't ask you anything else.'

He says nothing, but judging from his contrite expression, she knows she's hit the nail on the head. He's never been good at hiding his emotions either.

Isabelle Audoin. That's her name. Not that JB revealed it to her – in fact she hasn't seen him since the break-up; he left that very same afternoon. He had planned it all, anticipated everything. She found her on the internet by herself, after searching for roughly six minutes (turning on the computer took longer than the research itself). She remembered that he'd been to talk at a wine school in Beaune. There is only one wine school in Beaune, and it employs a dozen teachers, of whom only two are female. Their names are listed on its website, above photos of them among the vines. Catherine Cucq, tall, slim, seemingly fit (looks like she could do the Camino de Santiago) but in her fifties, with short hair and all skin and bone. Not JB's type. Unlike Isabelle Audoin, who is much younger, has perfect bone structure, as Patrick would say, looks outdoorsy and good with children. It's her, there's no doubt about it. She has the same kind of beauty as Clara but of a more dynamic, less romantic kind. The photo doesn't have a date so it's impossible to know when it was taken, but there's a triumphant look on her face that could very easily mean *I'm having a love affair with a handsome firefighter who looks like Flynn Rider, I'm having more sex than ever before, and I have never felt so fulfilled.*

It is a challenging and rather bizarre time. JB's departure and the incident with Madame Bach in the same week, one at either end of it.

Madame Bach is as tall as a tree, with long grey hair and glasses that give her bug eyes. She had once been a customer at the salon (during Audrey's time), then she started to come in less often, which didn't come as a surprise to anyone – they had noticed a change in her. One day they found out she was in Les Myosotis, a nursing home in the area. Madame Habib took her record off the little revolving stand, just as she does for deceased customers, and they forgot all about her large face with its sagging jowls.

Until this morning. It was still early, and Lorraine had only just sat down on her stool when they saw Madame Bach standing on the pavement outside the window of Cindy Coiffure, looking distressed. It was Nolwenn, looking up from her phone, who spotted her first.

'Oh, fudge.'

Oh, fudge, because Madame Bach was wearing a grey T-shirt emblazoned with the green Leroy Merlin triangle – and nothing else. No dress, no trousers, no tights, and no knickers. You could see what had happened: she had got out of bed at Les Myosotis and walked over without getting dressed for the day, probably without it even occurring to her.

Madame Habib went out onto the pavement and gave her a gown. She brought her inside and sat her down at the back of the salon, at Nolwenn's workstation. Madame Bach didn't seem to hear the questions they asked her, and she also appeared oblivious to the fact that she was holding a glass of water. She watched the women rushing around near her, a hazy look of surprise beginning to form on her face.

What had brought her to the salon? What in her subconscious made her choose this particular place? Perhaps it was a simple mistake, her mind blanking out several years and taking her back to one morning on a day she had an appointment there.

Madame Habib got in touch with the nursing home, who confirmed that she was *going out* more and more frequently. While they were waiting for the driver, Jacqueline asked Madame Bach if she wanted someone to do her hair. Receiving no reply, she decided that they'd wash it for her. And since neither Nolwenn nor Clara were free, she took off her bracelets, rolled up the sleeves of her cream-coloured satin blouse, and saw to the shampooing herself.

Naturally, she is starting to forget about Proust. JB and Isabelle Audoin are taking up all her headspace, even when she's on the bus, and the book has lain dormant at the bottom of her bag for several weeks. Then, one Sunday afternoon when she is supposed to be meeting her parents at the 'Washhouses of Burgundy' exhibition at the Museum of Photography, she decides to stay at home instead. She opens *The Guermantes Way* again, and Marcel makes his return. She remembers his brilliant intelligence and delicacy; she wonders how she has been managing without him and she begins to read avidly. Its pages offer the same solace, if not more, than that of chocolate or the sun, and she gets through 150 of them in three days.

It's very unlikely that you'd say to someone who's just been unexpectedly dumped after three and a half years, 'You should read *The Guermantes Way*.' You'd be more likely to suggest they sign up for the gym or get a cat, but that would be a mistake. Not the signing up for the gym or getting a cat part, but the failure to consider Proust. He may not have explicitly written a guide to surviving painful break-ups, but there is no one quite like Marcel for comforting the forsaken reader. He does this first of all by making them smarter, which is not insignificant, but also by making them realise that love does not exist, that it is just an invention of our brains in response to our own existential frustration and fear of abandonment, that the person we think we are in love with is nothing like who they are really, that we desire them because they elude us and that once we have them, we cannot remember what made us desire them, and that anyway, we are irredeemably alone, so in love, either we suffer terribly or we become bored to death.

Any regret at the loss of her relationship with JB is crushed before it can even take shape, as successfully as the spaceships of the Galactic Empire at the end of *Return of the Jedi*. And when, despite all of this, despite Proust, a pang of nostalgia manages to reach her heart, she just has to think about the final, affectionless ten months of their relationship, the large, pallid body of JB, which had become about as enticing as stewed tripe to a vegetarian, or even her dream of escaping to a secluded part of the countryside where she could read without video-game sound effects in the background or interruptions with questions about the time or what their next meal would be.

In the end, other people are the trickiest part, as is often the case with significant personal events. Her mother is so inordinately affected by JB's departure that you'd think it was she he had left. She has been verging on panic for several weeks, sending Clara texts that miss the point completely and usually start with *I've been thinking. I've been thinking, and you should write him a letter saying: 1) In life we all deserve a second chance (very important), and 2) If he agrees, say that you'd like to meet up to talk about things rationally* ... This is followed by a feeling of confusion that could have been sorted with a dose of magnesium, but will actually only be resolved later on a walk from Millau to the Tarn Gorges that has been organised by Annick's hiking club, over the course of which she discards the idea of having JB as a son-in-law like orange peel into a dustbin.

And of course, there's Madame Habib. Clara hadn't told her anything about what happened for several weeks, then one evening she finally spills the beans when they are both closing the salon. Jacqueline listens, taken in by the story, her lips trembling with emotion, staring fixedly at Clara with big, sad eyes. It has clearly conjured up a memory, reminding her of one, or several, previous break-ups. *But what are you going to do?* she stammers, as if Clara had just told her she'd lost everything in a fire. Then she lights a cigarette and declares with a weary sigh: *Oh, they really deserve to have their dicks cut off.*

One evening, however, she can't escape the feeling of sadness, as the film of what secretly happened at the wine school in Beaune plays out in her head. The first glance, the first words JB and Isabelle Audoin exchanged when they knew that things were becoming less professional. Where did it happen? In her classroom, after her lessons? In the Duster? Was it on JB's first or second visit? Clara knows the moves he would have made from experience, slow and then quick, the changes in his voice; she knows the taste and smell of his mouth, of his body. Did he kiss the soles of Isabelle Audoin's feet like he did Clara's? Did he embrace her big toe?

She gets up, takes half a sleeping pill from the bathroom, and goes back to bed.

How is it possible to miss someone who took up too much space when they were there? To be upset that you no longer have them when you no longer wanted them? What does she miss, exactly? Because she still wouldn't want to have him back . . .

Love isn't the same as love. And its loss isn't the same as its loss. As she stares at the ceiling, she imagines Proust saying this. *You have to see the positives, Mademoiselle*, she hears him add. *Now you've got the bed to yourself.* If she stands up, she thinks she will see him sitting in the armchair on the other side of the bedroom, head resting on his hand like in his famous portrait, and she hardly dares blink.

The next day, nothing – no inescapable feeling of sadness, and no Proustian ghost.

Her parents' names are Annick and Yves. *Annives and Yck*, as her Uncle Jacques used to say when she was little. He was Annick's secretive, practical-joker brother, and Clara had always been amused when he called them this, thinking it the height of humour and derision. It still puts a tender smile on Annick and Yves's faces, but JB did not find it funny. *Annives and Yck* – no, he really couldn't see why that made them laugh.

Now that he's gone, these kinds of memories come back to her like pieces of wood resurfacing, it no longer being necessary for her to push them underwater. Far from being insignificant, they are a perfect example of how differently they felt about things deep down, and how they would never have been in tandem.

She is at the bookshop, ordering *The Prisoner*. She hasn't finished *Sodom and Gomorrah* yet but is planning ahead.

'Are you reading all of *In Search of Lost Time*?'

She is fond of this bookseller. He reminds her of Ned Flanders, the Simpsons' neighbour – he is similarly normal and reassuring. Well, he's like a French Flanders, a little more attractive than the original, and with a bookshop that has black-and-white portraits of Beckett, Faulkner and Le Clézio on the walls.

'Yes, from the beginning.'

'For school or . . .?'

'No, just for myself. For pleasure.'

He looks at her in admiration. 'I don't know many young people who read it for pleasure. Of course, with all that TikTok stuff they can't concentrate for more than five seconds . . .' He taps away on his keyboard, his mind elsewhere. 'Proust is the best, that's for sure. Well, the entire twentieth century is unbeatable for literature. When you've got Céline, Colette . . .'

Clara smiles, relaxed. 'It's funny, all those female writers who were known by their first name.'

She thinks she hears someone behind her blow their nose. A woman has erupted into laughter. A customer who is waiting – and if Clara turned around, she would see the thick glasses, mop of fringed hair and greedy expression of someone who is already delighting in the idea of telling others what she's just heard.

Flanders waits a moment, then leans towards Clara and says, 'Céline is a man. His first name is Louis-Ferdinand.'

She feels herself turn as red as a beetroot, something that hasn't happened to her since school.

'Anyway, never mind,' the bookseller hastens to reassure her, looking at his computer as though he's talking to it. 'Shall we send you a text when it comes in, like normal?'

Lorraine has found a shrink: Marc Vauzelle, in Dijon. He doesn't do reimbursement forms, but he does tailor his fees to what his patients can afford. And the first session is free. She had her first one yesterday, and it's all she can talk about this morning. Is she convinced by it? Moved, more like. And she won't stop talking about it. *He says my dizzy spells are secret messages from my subconscious that we can decode together.* This is what she tells Madame Habib, who has recently started peppering her sentences with subtle 'hms'. *I didn't know what to tell him, so he said, 'Talk to me about your mother.' I replied, 'I can't see what she's got to do with my dizzy spells.' As soon as I said it, I saw my mother's face, the little bird-like look she had in her last days, and then* (she places her hand on Madame Habib's forearm) *I started to cry – to cry, my dear, and I couldn't stop!*

She has never read as much as she does now, particularly in the evenings – sometimes she turns out the light at two a.m., even on weekdays. Is it because it helps her forget that she's alone? Or is it that, quite simply, she now has more time to herself? The fact remains that the characters from the book – Françoise, the Guermantes family, Charlus – are becoming just as familiar to her as the people she sees every day. And sometimes, when she is tired and little things come back to her – a biting remark, the look of surprise on someone's face – she can't quite tell if she has experienced them or read about them.

Could it be that human nature is just lies, hypocrisy and mediocracy? That life is just a comedy of appearances that's about as funny as acid reflux? That nothing will ever live up to the desire that preceded it? That the only possible salvation, the only chance of happiness imaginable is to be found through connections with works of art?

It's a quiet morning at Cindy Coiffure. Clara has just finished with a customer and is looking at the appointment book. Her next one is at 10:45 a.m. – she has some time. She lifts her head and looks around the salon, whose entire length can be viewed from the till. Madame Habib is peering into one of the mirrors on the left, checking she doesn't have lipstick on her teeth. Nolwenn, who is also between appointments, is sweeping her workstation, her mind evidently somewhere else. Philippe Lavil's 'Il tape sur des bambous' is playing on Radio Nostalgie. It smells of Shalimar, L'Oréal hairspray and over-heated hair. The Cindy Coiffure microcosm. Clara sees it, understands it, *feels* it – and realises that it is no longer enough for her.

The volumes of *In Search of Lost Time* she has now read, in order of preference:

1   *The Guermantes Way*
2   *Swann's Way*
3   *Within a Budding Grove*
4   *Sodom and Gomorrah*

And the characters:

1   Françoise
2   Charlus
3   The grandmother
4   Swann and the Duchesse de Guermantes, tied

The last few thoughts she's recorded in her notebook:

Often, people in this book don't know that they're being watched (Charlus, the Duchesse de Guermantes, the grandmother).

It's sublime when he speaks to his grandmother on the phone (it's like he's speaking to her in the afterlife).

The book is as sensual and generous as a fruit, as a peach.

And the quotations:

The features of our face are hardly more than gestures which force of habit has made permanent.

The truth has no need to be uttered to be made apparent [. . .] one may perhaps gather it with more certainty, without waiting for words, without even bothering one's head about them, from a thousand outward signs, even from certain invisible phenomena, analogous in the sphere of human character to what in nature are atmospheric changes.

The still wet pavement changed by the sun into a golden lacquer.

Memories return to you when you are least expecting it. In fact, it's in the name – *involuntary memory*. The first time Clara experienced it was when she heard the lawnmower during her biology class, something she remembered a couple of months ago on the bus after she'd read the passage about the madeleine moment in *Swann's Way*. It happens again when she is at Marionnaud buying her father Givenchy Gentleman for his birthday. Somebody has sprayed Guerlain Habit Rouge next to her, and the smell wends its way to her nostrils. Habit Rouge is the perfume Clara gave JB the first Christmas they spent together, upon the advice of a salesperson who had assured her it was a *timeless classic*. In seconds she is transported back to an incredibly specific, incredibly *definite* period in her life. It all comes back to her: the sexual excess of that time (JB and she had sex wherever they could – on the train, in the swimming pool), the joy of exploring her Flynn Rider's body (his face was like this, his hips like that), the iron taste that their kisses would gradually take on, the pride she felt walking down the street with him and introducing him to friends and parents. And so too, almost more seductively, does the memory of days which were cold and cloudless, of parties to celebrate the forthcoming end of the year, and a general feeling of pleasure, light, confidence – being so young and beautiful, their lives could only be a resounding success.

It is an intense happiness that is laced with sorrow, or rather, a sorrow that is part and parcel of happiness. She closes her eyes and leans into what she is feeling, imagining that this will be the best way to make it pass. She also experiences a few more conscious thoughts – notably, that she had been more in love with JB and more affected by his absence than she'd like to admit. Her sister, who has come with her, puts an end to it:

'They're out of Gentleman. We'll have to come back on Tuesday. Gutted.'

She laughs to herself all alone on the bus from Palais-de-Justice to République, thinking about when the Duchesse de Guermantes says a young man looks like a tapir.

She's in the middle of drying Madame Fabre's hair when Madame Habib comes over to her and whispers in her ear, with all the secrecy of sharing a PIN code, 'Phone for you. Claudie Hansen.'

Clara switches off the hairdryer. 'Does she want to change the date of her appointment?'

Jacqueline accidentally lets out a little burp that she covers with a subtle *pff*, meaning there is a short pause before she replies. 'I don't think so; she wouldn't need to talk to you to do that.'

It has been a busy day, not without its irritations. Clara slopes over to the till and picks up the phone, wondering what could possibly happen next. 'Hello, Claudie.'

'Ah, Clara, sorry to bother you, you must be very busy . . .' Her voice is both deep and delicate. Hearing it on a day like today is like catching sight of a familiar face in a crowd. 'I'm calling because I've had an idea. I know I have an appointment next week, but it can't wait. It came to me yesterday evening and I can't stop thinking about it; I even talked to Michèle about it, and she agrees with me. Anyway, I'll stop beating around the bush. I think you should read Proust.'

She's been reading Proust for almost nine months; that's why

Claudie invited her over. They talked about it all afternoon, and at dinner too. She is starting to think that Claudie is losing the plot, but then she hears her clarify: 'Read it *to other people*. Out loud. Yesterday evening when I was putting away my CDs, I could hear you reading out the blurb of the one we listened to at mine. D'you remember? When you came over, I gave you the CD and you read the first few sentences of the blurb ... Your voice, Clara, is just as gentle, just as delicate, as the text. Your voice is like the scent of the hawthorn.'

Those words, in this setting. Her brain stops working, and she can't think of anything more interesting to say than *That's nice* and again *That's nice*, then *Good afternoon*, then she ends the call.

She feels something quivering inside her as she puts the phone back in its cradle, and it doesn't let up. She goes back to her workstation, where Madame Habib is keeping Madame Fabre company, but she doesn't stop. She walks past the two women and takes refuge in the back room, then goes out into the courtyard behind the salon. The sky is white, electric; she grimaces, then she crouches down and starts to cry. Everything that needs to come out comes out. JB leaving; feeling humiliated at the bookshop; Isabelle Audoin and Madame Bach; increasingly difficult days at the salon; this book that is throwing everything into question; and now the idea that she must read to people. And there's another thing. She has recently been watching videos of people from Proust's time on YouTube, the ordinary people of 1900–1910 with their umbrellas and top hats. She sees them rushing around Avenue de l'Opéra and outside Notre-Dame and she feels great pity for them because she knows something they don't know yet, which is that nothing lasts, that all lives are forgotten and the memory of them will vanish just as quickly as a drawing traced on a steamed-up window.

She needs to stop; she'll never be able to go back to work. But it's strange: the more she cries, the more she needs to cry, and now she's also whimpering like a small animal, something she realises when the door opens and out comes Madame Habib. She kneels and takes Clara in her arms, saying, 'It will be alright, sweetheart . . . it will be alright.'

III

CLARA

'And with that old, intermittent fatuity, which reappeared in him now that he was no longer unhappy, and lowered, at the same time, the average level of his morality, he cried out in his heart: "To think that I have wasted years of my life, that I have longed for death, that the greatest love that I have ever known has been for a woman who did not please me, who was not in my style!'

She closes the book, clears her throat and waits a moment, not daring to look at Madame Renaud.

It hadn't gone well. She'd said *control* instead of *console*, meaning the sentence didn't make sense, and she'd skipped an entire line in the second section (the text is very dense). She apologised, then picked herself back up and read to the end without feeling any of it, pronouncing the words just as they appeared on the page.

Madame Renaud looks unimpressed. Obviously. She is staring into space, moving her lips slightly without making a sound. Claudie introduced her to Clara as *an old friend and Proust fan who'd like to hear the end of 'Swann in Love'*. She should have added, *and she'll make you very uncomfortable if things don't go well...*

'Where are you parked?' she asks, finally.

'I walked.'

'Do you live close by?'

She is trying not to pass comment on what she's just heard, and she is right. Clara plays along.

'No, I live in Les Chavannes. I came here straight from the salon, which is behind Place de la Libération.'

'I see. And how do you get home?'

'From the salon, I get the bus. The three.'

'Ah yes, the three.'

'It goes straight there. I'm lucky.'

'Yes, that's handy.'

They'd said as much as they could about the matter and there was nothing more to it. The old woman got up from her armchair, holding tightly onto it as she did so, and they both silently went out into a corridor that smelled like a hospital. As they were walking, Clara spotted in the living room, on a highly polished sideboard, a photo of the pope framed in silver. By the time they got to the front door she was fighting the urge to cry.

'Goodbye, then.'

'Yes, see you tomorrow.'

'Sorry?'

'I said *See you tomorrow*.'

'To . . . read?'

'Well, yes. Claudie and I talked about two sessions. *Swann in Love* and the grandmother's death. Didn't she tell you?'

'Yes, but my reading wasn't . . . Did you like it?'

'Of course. Or I wouldn't be asking you to come back.'

'I made a mistake at one point.'

'Oh, maybe; I didn't notice. You have a lovely tone to your voice. It rises and falls and is very nice to listen to. And you don't overact, which is good. The last person I had read Proust as if it were a Brazilian telenovela, I couldn't believe it . . . So, tomorrow at seven thirty, same as today?'

'Agreed.'

Madame Renaud takes her arm. 'I'm looking after my granddaughter tomorrow afternoon; my daughter is dropping her off after lunch. She's four years old and she can't sit still; she draws on everything. I like her very much but a whole afternoon is far too long. Knowing that you're coming afterwards will bolster my spirits.'

On her way back she listens to a song on repeat, which she'd heard at the salon. This time, she didn't forget. 'Don't Stop Me Now' by Queen plays in her ears as she walks diagonally across Place de la Libération and then through the old town, passing the cathedral on the way.

The key is to go slowly. It reduces the risk of stuttering or slipping into reading without thinking about it, and, most importantly, it allows the person listening to appreciate the text in all its charm.

Take the sentence *The Marquis de Palancy, his face bent downwards at the end of his long neck, his round bulging eye glued to the glass of his monocle, was moving with a leisurely displacement through the transparent shade and appeared no more to see the public in the stalls than a fish that drifts past, unconscious of the press of curious gazers, behind the glass wall of an aquarium.* As a listener, it is difficult to miss the image of the fish in its aquarium, even if it's been read too quickly. But on the other hand, if the reader doesn't give you enough time to hear the words *his long neck, his face bent downwards* or *the transparent shade*, they will probably go over your head, which would be a shame.

Proust's commas seem like they have been placed at random, and they are poorly suited to reading such long sentences out loud. And so, Clara starts adding marks that only she will understand to the passages she is preparing to read: a / between certain words to indicate a pause; and a // between certain sentences to suggest a longer pause, so she can get her breath back and give the person listening time to understand what they've just heard (you shouldn't be afraid of pauses: a silence always seems longer to the person reading than to the person listening).

Other marks soon begin to adorn the pages of her books: a >> in the margin means she can speed up without running the risk of stuttering (in lists or in speech, for example); a ~ just above the gap between two words shows she can link their sounds (linking the sounds between words when you shouldn't is the easiest trap to fall into when reading); and a line, a simple black line, underneath a word, shows she wants to emphasise it. Like *a shudder* in the sentence *a shudder ran through my whole body, and I stopped, intent upon the extraordinary changes that were taking place*, or *disillusionments* in *Life in withdrawing from her had taken with it the disillusionments of life*.

These marks are a bit like signs left along walking trails, indispensable to those who find them but of no use to an experienced guide, who doesn't even notice them any more. She finds them helpful during her preparation, and even more so later, once she has read and reread the text to get a hold on it, and memorised the rhythm and intonation she wants to bring to it. She can then devote herself to the most important thing while she's reading: just being with the words. Because that is by far the most difficult part: being *within* the text and staying put, all the way from the first syllable to the last, so a ringing phone, a baby crying or even a pressure cooker exploding in the room next door wouldn't put her off reading. Like yoga.

It's been a while since they last saw Madame de Lamballe at the salon, and for good reason: she had a stroke. This morning she made a return. Madame Habib made a fuss over her and Nolwenn did her hair. She is walking a little unsteadily; one side of her face is less responsive than the other and she no longer uses verbs, expressing herself using purely concepts and onomatopoeias. *My daughter head in the clouds, her trainers on the stairs, my son-in-law crash bang, night in A & E.* Or *Lisbon, salt cod and potato mash, little custard tarts, ouillouillouille the weight!* It certainly makes her outbursts a little silly, but it also makes them sound like haikus whose meaning you can easily work out. Either way, nobody said anything after she left, Madame Habib out of propriety and Nolwenn because she had started doing something else. Meanwhile, Clara imagined what poor old Madame de Lamballe's quirk would have inspired in Proust . . . And to top it all off, she's a baroness!

The cat has been radically transformed by JB's departure. He tried to find JB at first, seeming even more away with the fairies than usual; he would go into the bedroom and look around JB's side of the bed as if he'd just landed on Mars, or stare at the hook where JB used to leave his sports bag, unable to understand why there was nothing there. And one evening, when Clara got home, she found him on the sofa (which had thus far been reserved for humans), purring (something also hitherto unseen), eyes closed in contentment and tail gently wagging. He had obviously realised that JB wasn't coming back, that it was just him and Clara from now on – and clearly, that suited him just fine.

SURNAME:
Poitrenaud

NAME:
Clara

DATE AND PLACE OF BIRTH:
29 March 1997, Dole

PROPOSED ACTIVITY:
Reading of extracts from In Search of Lost Time *by Marcel Proust*

FIELD (delete as appropriate):
~~Theatre~~   ~~Music~~   ~~Dance~~   ~~Circus skills~~
~~Art installation~~   ~~Sound installation~~   ~~Digital installation~~

OTHER (please specify):
Public reading

'Ten days?'

'Do you think that's too many?'

'I mean, Patrick will be off on the same days.'

'Only in the first week.'

'Yes, but Patrick's only in on Saturdays.'

'Nolwenn will be in. All ten days.'

'Sure, but that won't stop some of our customers potentially going somewhere else. I don't want to hand Mariella Brunella business on a plate.'

'Well, there aren't so many people around at the end of July.'

'That remains to be seen … Do you really need all that time off? The festival's only four days long.'

'Yes, but I have to prepare. That's what I'm going to do for the first few days. Learn my lines, at home.'

'Can't you do it in the evenings after work?'

'No, I'm always knackered. And I also go and read to a lady at her house three times a week.'

'Claudie Hansen?'

'No – one of her friends. Well, a friend of her mother. Madame

Renaud, who lives on Avenue de Paris. I was originally only meant to do it the once, but she wanted me to come back, and now I go there three times a week.'

'To read?'

'Yes, to read Proust to her. It's a passion of hers.'

'See, that's your practice.'

'For what?'

'The festival.'

'Oh, yeah. But it will be different.'

'Do you get stage fright?'

'No. Well, I don't know; I've never thought about it before.'

'That reminds me of when I was younger; my sister and I sometimes got jobs as receptionists at motor and aeronautical shows. Our boss told us to show off our legs. Every time she walked past us, she would suddenly hike up our skirts. I saw Gilbert Bécaud. You know, the singer. He signed his autograph on a Kleenex – that's all I had on me. The pen leaked and his autograph was illegible . . . I don't know why I'm telling you this, it's irrelevant.'

'Yes . . . So, I can take two weeks off in July?'

'Yes, Clara, take two weeks off in July to read Marcel Proust. We'll manage.'

Lorraine comes to the salon with a book now, in addition to the coffees: *Five Lectures on Psychoanalysis* by Sigmund Freud, recommended to her by Vauzelle. After the usual exchange of news with Madame Habib, she perches on the stool and dives into her book, making sure everyone present can see the title and name of its author. And so there are two readers at Cindy Coiffure: one of Proust and the other of Freud, which is simultaneously very classy and rather puzzling.

Clara has also noticed that Lorraine, an elegant woman, is even more so on the days she is seeing her shrink (a low-cut dress instead of her usual trousers, and an ice-blue jean jacket that complements her blonde hair) and she doesn't ever, ever talk about hanging herself any more.

It's opening time on a Saturday. Two customers are already waiting; they must be quick. In the courtyard behind the salon, eyes still puffy with sleep, Patrick issues Clara a warning: 'Alright, don't be too surprised.'

He wedges his cigarette into the corner of his mouth and unfurls a poster. Clara looks at it, her hand clapped over her mouth.

It is a black-and-white drawing that produces the visual equivalent of nails scratching a chalkboard. There's a young woman with manga-style features and a plunging neckline; she looks like she's winking, unless something went wrong when it came to drawing her face. Below and to the left is a profile done in Chinese ink, probably of Proust, which brings to mind Jack the Ripper or a criminal of the same ilk. And at the very top, on the right, in a font that is more suggestive of the world of *Game of Thrones* than that of *In Search of Lost Time*, is written 'Clara Reads Proust'.

Needless to say, although she is familiar with Patrick's drawing style, she'd had something else in mind. Patrick notices this and explains his work, as if it were *Guernica* or the *Oath of the Horatii*:

'I told myself that the people who know Proust will come anyway, so the young people are the ones you'll need to attract. That's why it's in manga style. I wanted to give Proust a new lease of life, shake off his stuck-up image.'

'Well, it's certainly not stuck-up.'

'But do you like it?'

Clara folds her arms over her chest. 'I like the title,' she says, pointing at it.

'Yeah, I've forgotten what you told me to write . . .'

'"Reading of extracts from *In Search of Lost Time* by Marcel Proust."'

'Ah yes, but that was too long. "Clara Reads Proust" is better. Well, I think it is. It's memorable.'

'Definitely.'

He rubs his eye, irritated by the cigarette smoke, and says, 'It'll bring you luck, you'll see.'

'Thank you very much.' She considers adding *really* but stops herself.

'What on earth are you both doing? Everyone's waiting for you.' Nolwenn has poked her head out into the courtyard. 'What's that?' she says, indicating the poster.

Patrick, who has just rolled it up, unrolls it once more. Nolwenn comes closer to get a better look. Her eyes dart from the poster to Patrick and quickly back again, lingering on the drawing for as long as possible.

'Did you do that?'

'Yes – why? D'you like it?'

She swallows. 'Honestly, I love it.'

149

Raymonde's Story, Conclusion

I must point out that this thing with Bernard and me didn't come out of nowhere. I had always liked him; he even flirted with me when we were younger. Except I was already with René, I got pregnant, and we had to get married – anyway, nothing happened. But I still thought about him. Over the years I've taken a disproportionate amount of pleasure in going to his butcher's. Saturday mornings when there was a queue were my favourite because I could look at him for longer. I could see his beautifully shaped nose, his well-maintained nails, his hair which curled a little at the ends, and it made me feel warm inside. I ended up buying a lot of meat. So much that I wonder if that might be why everyone in my family is diabetic (meat with every meal – I'm not sure it's the best diet). I must also point out that Bernard is single. He has been since his wife went off with another woman about fifteen years ago. The two women lived in Dijon at first and then left to live on some island, I can't remember where – that was a funny story, too. And there I am, asking to spend a night with him. To my mind, it was so I could say to René: You dipped your wick, and now I've also had some fun (sorry about the choice of words, Jacqueline, I'm just saying what pops into my head). Except things never go as planned. Bernard says yes (oh, that's not what I'm surprised about – I don't know any man who'd turn down that kind of offer, and at sixty-seven years of age, I'm not over the hill yet either). No, the surprising thing is that it's going so well. For a start, the meal was delicious. We went to a restaurant in Crissey; I had duckling with cranberries and Bernard had a rack of lamb. We were really enjoying ourselves, then we went to a nearby bed and breakfast to spend the night. We didn't do anything crazy; it was even better than that. We lay down on the bed and started to talk. Bernard rubbed my back while he listened to me; the window was open, and you could hear the birds all night long. Every now and then I fell asleep for a while, and I was woken up by him kissing my neck or forehead. I opened my eyes and saw this man looking at me, telling me he was content – what more could you want? After that, going home to tell the other one he could come back to the house was neither here nor there. René can come back, leave, marry his Chinese woman if he wants; I don't give two hoots. All I do is think about Bernard, his mouth, his skin; I await the little messages he sends me from the butcher's during the day, and I count down the days until our next meeting. Yes, because we are planning to meet up on Saturday. For two days, this time, which we will spend at the Lac des Settons. Incidentally, that's why I'm here. I've brought a photo that I found somewhere or other, I was wondering if I could have the same thing done. Hair a bit lighter, you see, tied up at the back but with a little bit coming loose at the front. I was thinking Patrick or Clara could do it for me.

The location is unclear – or rather, it changes, transforms. It starts in the passage that houses Cindy Coiffure and then moves to the hallway of a building whose floors suddenly disappear, giving way to a starry sky.

The bookseller who looks like Flanders asks her what the Baron de Charlus's first name is. *Palamède!* she replies straight away, before overexcitedly adding: *And Mémé is his nickname!*

Her interlocuter nods and continues, 'More difficult now. Whose first name is Bathilde in *In Search of Lost Time*?'

'The grandmother!'

'Very impressive!'

Seamlessly (perhaps because she got the answer right), Clara finds herself thrown into infinite space, floating among the debris and other remnants of silvery stars. She can make out a figure in the distance, a figure who is as confused as she is, it is a man who is coming towards her: it is Proust. Their bodies gently interlock and slowly swirl in cosmic nothingness. Very quickly they are naked, the tiniest portion of her skin touching the writer's own smooth skin; it is an unspeakable pleasure. Every time he moves his pelvis, their legs graze or he applies pressure with his hands, they move one step closer to ecstasy. This progression is accompanied by a tune that gets louder and louder, in fact it's not really a tune but three single notes that sound like a spoon tapping glasses full of water; it's a phone, it's her phone waking her up – it's seven a.m. on 21 July, the first day of the festival.

As she's reaching out to pick up her phone, and even after she's silenced her alarm, she thinks about how strange it is that aside from his literary talent, nobody talks about the fact that Proust was a truly exceptional lover.

She finds her spot on Rue des Tonneliers, outside the white painted shop front of an old jeweller's. She had been here before, ten days ago, with the person running the fringe festival. She tapes her poster to a no-entry sign, and, above it, staples a piece of paper detailing what she will read:

11 a.m.: Swann gets over Odette
3 p.m.: The train journey and the girl selling coffee and milk
6 p.m.: The Vinteuil Sonata

She sits down on a rattan stool next to it, opposite three rugs arranged in a semi-circle, which Anaïs had helped her bring in her Citroën Saxo, and she waits. She waits, but nobody comes. *Not even a layabout*, as Madame Habib would say. It is twenty to eleven, twelve minutes to eleven, three minutes to eleven, and she has never felt so alone.

On the other side of the high street, some kids from Le Creusot are breakdancing, and they've got a good five or six spectators. It isn't that many, but she'd be so happy if five or six people were sitting in front of her. Except everyone is walking straight past her, and whether they're on their own, with their partners or with their families, they all have the same reaction. They look at the poster, the programme, and then they look at Clara, and by the time they've see her it's too late; they've already made their decision: they aren't interested. Their apologetic expressions say it all. *We're sure you read very well, and we appreciate the effort you've gone to, but 'Swann gets over Odette' just isn't for us.* They think the enthusiastic young woman reading Proust at the street festival is charming, but they're not interested – it just doesn't appeal to them. They'd rather stop and watch the breakdancers, because spinning around like that is really quite something, or else buy an ice cream at the tearoom near the cathedral, even though the weather's a bit unpredictable, because ice cream is so delicious.

It's five past eleven and she isn't about to start reading by herself, out loud to nobody – that would be pathetic. So, she puts on a brave face and goes over lines that she knows almost by heart, forcing a half-smile in case anyone looks at her. How could she have thought this would work? It's better to stick to doing normal things. Being a hairdresser is a good choice: you do it for five out of seven days, you get a salary at the end of the month, then you do the same thing the next month. It has meaning, significance for both hairdresser and customer, while setting up in the middle of the road hoping people will come and sit on rugs to listen to extracts from *In Search of Lost Time* is completely out of step with today's world. There is no visible, Instagrammable outcome – unlike breakdancing, or two scoops of Madagascan vanilla ice cream beautifully presented in a little tub.

Eleven minutes past eleven. Nobody. That's enough humiliation for her. She picks up her bag and asks the man selling oriental pastries on the pavement opposite to watch her things, then starts walking down the road.

She spots Flanders frowning at his screen in the bookshop, which by some twist of fate is about twenty metres from where she is reading. A little further along, some actors are putting on a comedy play from the windows of a building; they take turns appearing on the ground floor and first floor as they say their lines. She stops and watches them, smiling for the first time that day. They make her feel better because they are funny, but also because they are performing for only one person apart from her, and yet they still look happy. It isn't really a play, more like a succession of short sketches. When one finishes, she claps and carries on walking in the direction of the Saône.

On Rue Saint-Georges, a boy sitting against a wall is playing an instrument unlike anything she has seen before. It's like a small flying saucer made of metal and dotted with holes, each of which produces a different note when struck. From the instrument he is drawing a melody that sounds almost Hawaiian and is delicate and somewhat bewitching, yet people are walking straight past him as well. She stops, listens to him, watches him. The look of concentration on his face, his long, precise hands, and even his completely unremarkable toes in sandals have a calming, sensual effect on her. Her early morning dream comes back to her; she remembers her body being intertwined with Proust's, the feel of his smooth skin, and realises that it's been a while since she last had sex. The musician must have sensed something because he looks up and smiles at her, continuing to play all the while. She hesitates, moves away, and stumbles upon a magnificent harlequin on stilts. A black mask decorated with white feathers and a costume the colour of Christmas sweets. He leans towards her as she walks past and begins to follow her. She picks up her pace and he lets her go, looking disappointed.

She likes this slightly strange, creative atmosphere, she thinks, as she approaches the quays. She was clearly supposed to experience the festival as a spectator rather than as an artist. It was a signal failure, an error in casting. She will call the person in charge of the fringe festival to ask if it's possible to pull out and not come back in the afternoon. They will be sure to understand, given that her first reading had zero spectators.

She sits on a bench next to the Saône. Her eyes linger on the bank opposite, then on a couple of joggers who are coming towards her from the right: a man and woman running next to each other, whom she recognises straight away. JB and Isabelle Audoin. She immediately grabs her bag and buries her head inside it, pretending she's searching for something. But as they run past, she can't help herself from quickly looking up. They are both focused on jogging and pay her no attention, but she notices two things. Firstly, JB has put on weight. Oh, just a bit, but enough for it to show, in between his hips and his upper thighs. It doesn't look great. Secondly, the girl with him is clearly not Isabelle Audoin. She is blonde with a ponytail and is incredibly slim, apart from her breasts and bottom. Nothing like the adorable teacher at the wine school in Beaune, whom, completely unbeknown to her, Clara had blamed for the failure of her relationship. Life has a funny way of working out.

She eats plain sushi for lunch, and then, as she's walking back to Rue des Tonneliers, she calls the festival organiser, who tells her that no, she can't pull out on the first day; it wouldn't be fair to the committee that chose her, that reading Proust will of course attract fewer people than breakdancing but it makes her stand out; it sets her apart from the rest, that she was just talking about her to a freelance journalist friend at the *Journal de Saône-et-Loire* and said *You should talk to the girl who's reading Proust* and that this friend replied that she'd try to put something in Saturday's paper, which would be ideal since the festival doesn't really get going until the weekend . . .

Somebody is sitting on the rugs.

It is two fifty-seven; it can't be a coincidence – someone sitting down because they are sick of walking around. No, he is obviously waiting for the reader, waiting for the reading to begin.

They politely acknowledge one another. She sits down, realises that she has stage fright, and remembers Madame Habib asking her a question about this very topic. Still, it is her first time reading in public. She takes her book and a little bottle of water out of her bag, clears her throat and addresses her one and only spectator: 'I will now read an extract from *Within a Budding Grove*. It is a passage I like very much. We are on the train with the main character and his grandmother, going to Balbec on the Normandy coast.'

The person sitting down, a slim, tanned man in his sixties who must be a cyclist, nods, and instead of listening, asks, 'Do you like Fabrice Luchini?'

She can't see the relevance of the question but says *yes*, putting a finger to her lips at the same time to encourage him to be quiet. She opens the book, closes her eyes for a moment to clear her mind and centre herself, in this place and time, and begins: '*Sunrise is a necessary concomitant of long railway journeys, just as are hard-boiled eggs, illustrated papers, packs of cards . . .*'

Hearing her own reading voice feels like being reunited with a very dear friend. A warmth floods through her, a force; the feeling that when she is reading out loud to other people, nothing bad can happen to her. She was made to do this, to help people to hear the musicality of words; she can no longer doubt it.

'*The scenery became broken, abrupt, the train stopped at a little station between two mountains . . .*'

(A young woman with rosy cheeks is about to appear and offer the train passengers coffee and milk. When he sees her, Marcel will experience a taste of beauty and happiness, going as far as to imagine how wonderful it might be to spend his life with her, watching her as she goes about her daily tasks. Clara adores this radiant evocation, unclear as it is to her whether it corresponds to a dream or to a memory.)

'. . . *Above her body, which was of massive build, the complexion of her face was so burnished and so ruddy that she appeared almost as though I were looking at her through a lighted window.*'

Two slashes in the margin invite her to pause for a moment.

She looks up to gauge her spectator's reaction to her reading, but he has disappeared. When? She pays this no attention; she can just as easily read to nobody for two minutes. Well, not nobody exactly, since the man selling oriental pastries is standing on his doorstep, arms folded over the apron that hides his large belly. He greets her with a nod before going back inside, and she takes a moment, book resting on her thighs, shoulders relaxed, thinking about nothing in particular . . .

'You alright?' A girl who was walking down the street stops next to her.

'Meh.'

'You look completely . . .'

'There's no one here. There was someone but . . .'

She doesn't have the strength to go on.

The girl comes and sits down in front of her, on the rugs. She is small and brunette with beautiful doe-like eyes and a strong chin. She is wearing a khaki vest top and smells faintly of sweat.

'The first day is always dead. People don't dare stop anywhere. They find the things they're interested in and plan to come back. For what it's worth, we're not even performing today. We're starting tomorrow. But even tomorrow it will be dead. It kicks off on Friday.'

'Are you in a play?'

'Yes. At Port Nord, with a theatre company. *Merry Christmas and a Happy End of the World*, that's what it's called. You might've seen posters for it. It's more of an experience than a play. We get the audience to walk around what we think a post-apocalyptic world might be like.'

'Wow.'

'I'm Mathilde.'

'Clara.'

They shake hands.

'Clara who reads Proust . . .'

'Yes. Well, not that much this morning.'

'That'll change,' says Mathilde, picking up *Within a Budding Grove*, which she flicks through before commenting: 'I've never attempted Proust. It's like Dostoyevsky and stuff like that. I'm intimidated, to be honest.'

'You shouldn't be.'

'Isn't it . . . *heavy*?'

'It's actually pretty light. At least, I think so. I glide through it.'

Mathilde picks a passage at random, reads it to herself and then out loud, carefully enunciating the syllables: '*Grief that is caused one by a person with whom one is in love can be bitter, even when it is interpolated among preoccupations, occupations, pleasures in which that person is not directly involved and from which our attention is diverted only now and again to return to it . . .* It's philosophy, really.'

Clara smiles. 'Doesn't it make you feel good?'

'I'm not sure, I'll need to think about that,' laughs Mathilde.

She gives the book back and then there's a silence, during which Clara looks at the building opposite, and in particular at a chimney right at the top, which is bathed in an incandescent yellow in the newly appeared sun.

'Come.' Mathilde, now standing up, offers her hand. 'I'm taking you away.'

'Where?'

'It's a secret.'

Clara gets up. 'I have a reading at six o'clock.'

'You'll be back in time.'

'I'll have to ask the gentleman opposite to watch my stuff.'

She asks the gentleman opposite to watch her stuff and then they walk down the street, side by side. They look like sisters.

She has only ever seen Port Nord from a distance. It is a spectacular industrial wasteland, a landscape of metal ruins, shacks with broken glass roofs and greenish pools that are almost definitely toxic. The cranes and gangways look like skeletons in the sky, and the air causes the pulleys to screech, making it sound as though someone is shouting. Right in the centre of this nightmare scene, a group of artists have set up in an old warehouse. Inside is a saloon piano, a clothes rail of theatre costumes on wheels, a wooden crate full of artichokes, a bike suspended from the ceiling and a selection of doors in different colours, which are probably used for sets. But the space is completely deserted this afternoon; everything is happening outside, on the large wooden terrace by the entrance. There, among a confusion of tables and benches, you can play the guitar; you can talk while stubbing out your cigarette in a little stainless-steel ashtray; you can sit thinking to yourself in a corner with your arms around your crossed legs, gazing into the Saône which flows past just a few metres away. To Clara, this is a revelation. It is possible to live differently; there are other options: you don't have to go out every day and cut, curl and perm the hair of women you wouldn't otherwise meet in a million years.

'This is Clara,' says Mathilde, to no one in particular. 'She's reading Proust on Rue des Tonneliers.'

The guitar falls silent; people look up, turn around; a *Hi, Clara* rings out. As she gives them a little wave, she notices someone she recognises. The musician from earlier that morning. He is there in front of her, right in front of her, as if it had been planned. He has just rolled a cigarette and one bare foot is resting on the bench. He is smiling exactly as he did on Rue Saint-Georges. He is tall, slim, borderline skinny.

Mathilde asks Clara what she'd like to drink. *A beer*, she replies, and then she meets the gaze of the musician, who motions for her to come and sit down opposite him. The guitar starts up again. The weather is perfectly lovely. The Saône, in the sun, is sparkling like an opal.

She can't have had any more than forty minutes' sleep last night, and yet she doesn't feel tired at all. For the past hour she has been stopping friendly-looking passers-by on Rue des Tonneliers. *Madame, have you heard of Proust?* or *Now you, something tells me you like Marcel Proust.* And when no one else walks past, she starts again on Rue aux Fèvres. *When I say 'Swann's Way', what do you think of?* People are indulging her: they are out walking; they are on holiday; she is young and pretty.

Yesterday evening at Port Nord, Mathilde and the others told her she had to go out and find her audience. *Grab them by the scruff of the neck, like a cat and its kittens.* Especially with the activity she's chosen. Aside from a few Proust superfans, people are very unlikely to come of their own accord to sit on her rugs and listen to a reading called *The train journey and the girl selling coffee and milk*. They have to be told how beautiful the prose is, and about the pleasure they will get and the satisfaction they will feel in the future when they hear mention of Swann, Charlus or Guermantes and know who they are.

And when she has a gap between readings, she can't just stay sitting there, staring at the chimneys of the rooftop opposite or gossiping with the man selling oriental pastries. She has to do her own publicity. By handing out flyers, for example – postcard-size copies of the poster Patrick designed, of which she ordered 500 from the printing shop.

She does everything with surprising ease, with noticeable, infectious enjoyment. She is stimulated by the nights without much sleep, and there is a fire burning within her which obliterates any fear. She feels transported by the evening she has just had, the people she met, their creativity. By the reading she did for them just after midnight, in the flickering light of the candles positioned at each of the terrace's four corners, of one of her favourite passages from *In Search of Lost Time* – it is one of the funniest and most cruel, when the Guermantes are leaving for a society dinner and pay almost no attention to Swann, who has just told them he has a terminal illness. *You're as strong as the Pont Neuf. You'll live to bury us all!* Not to mention the time she spent after that with Paolo, the handsome hang-drum player, under a glass roof in a part of the warehouse that reminded her of the cabin of a boat, their words turning into caresses as daylight started to glow.

Her publicity campaign is bearing fruit. Eight people (a veritable crowd) come to her reading at eleven a.m. She certainly makes an impression, kicking off the day with *The madeleine moment.*

'No sooner had the warm liquid, and the crumbs with it, touched my palate than a shudder ran through my whole body, and I stopped, intent upon the extraordinary changes that were taking place …'

Twenty minutes of joy, at the end of which the applause rings out on Rue des Tonneliers.

At three o'clock, there aren't quite as many people – five when she starts reading and six by the end, which is to be expected. The streets start emptying out after lunch before they fill up again, and the passage she is reading isn't as well known as *The madeleine moment* either: it is *Odette appears on Avenue du Bois*.

'*Suddenly, on the gravelled path, unhurrying, cool, luxuriant, Mme Swann appeared, displaying around her a toilet which was never twice the same, but which I remember as being typically mauve ...*'

When she looks up from reading, she sees that someone is filming her on their phone. She feels a sense of joy, a shimmering, and this happens several times over the course of this magical day. There's the person who walks past and yells: *It takes cojones to read Proust in the street!* There's Flanders, who comes and tells her he'd sold two copies of *Swann's Way* before lunchtime. *You're going to bump Proust's sales with your readings!*

And later, there's the gift, the reward, of spotting Madame Habib, Nolwenn and Patrick among the dozen people who have come to listen to *How memories work* at six o'clock. Jacqueline looks as chic as someone invited to a presentation of the Légion d'honneur at the Élysée Palace, Patrick is wearing a black T-shirt emblazoned with the words 'I'd rather be dead', and Nolwenn waves at her. Clara is gripped by an emotion, which she holds at a distance while she reads.

'... *the better part of our memory exists outside ourself, in a blatter of rain, in the smell of an unaired room or of the first crackling brushwood fire in a cold grate: wherever, in short, we happen upon what our mind, having no use for it, had rejected ...*'

After which, all four of them come together.

'I didn't understand it all, but you read very well; it's like you've been doing it your whole life.' (Nolwenn)

'You're just *the best*. Does anyone want a drink?' (Patrick)

'What didn't you understand?' (Madame Habib, to Nolwenn)

'Nothing. Well, everything. It's written in a complicated way, I think.' (Nolwenn)

'It's very simple, in fact. He's saying that the things that bring back memories best are the details you've remembered without realising it, like the smell of a bedroom or a fire.' (Madame Habib)

'No one wants a drink?' (Patrick)

And now they are sitting on the terrace of a café on Rue Saint-Vincent, with the setting sun leaving half of their faces in shadow. Madame Habib, who is feeling relaxed after an Americano cocktail, starts talking about her parents, which has never happened before. She doesn't know who her father is; she was raised by her mother and her aunts, and Clara realises that her fear of abandonment is not so much that of an adult as that of a child who has seen the women around her abandoned and handed over to fate. Patrick is listening to her, attentive, taking a drag on a cigarette that he spent an inordinate amount of time rolling. Nolwenn is absent-mindedly watching people walk down the narrow street, before taking everyone by surprise with an announcement:

'I have something to tell you all.'

There's silence around the two small tables; everyone is expecting something terrible.

'I passed my test,' she says, in the same tone of voice as someone telling you the time.

'Your . . . driving test?' asks Patrick.

Nolwenn nods. 'I took another one without telling anyone because I thought I was going to fail again. But I passed.'

'Well, now!' says Madame Habib, who, emotional and un-inhibited thanks to the Americano, turns to her left to take her employee in her arms. 'I'm so proud of you.'

Clara raises her glass to Nolwenn.

'Bravo,' she smiles, just before her eye happens to be caught by a tall, dark-haired man who comes to their table, leans over and kisses her on the neck.

Paolo has come to join them, with his mini flying saucer, his beautiful heavy-lidded eyes and his easy-going manner. Paolo, who woke her up this morning singing 'Águas de Março' to her, tracing the contours of her face with his index finger. He talks about how hot it is, about the coming weekend and about a slightly mad tourist who'd whispered *I'd marry you right now* in his ear while he was playing. Clara listens, watching the others. It's stupid, but for the whole time, and for no precise reason, perhaps because she's had such a good day that won't ever be repeated and that as it goes by is in some ways already over, she really has to try to hold back her tears.

IV

EPILOGUE

She'll have to tell her

They were meant to go straight to the hotel from the station, but just before they arrived, Isabella said she wanted to see the hair salon where her mother had once worked. This story has always intrigued her. When she was little, she would even tell it to people who hadn't asked. *My mother used to be a hairdresser.* Nowadays, those who know Clara are usually familiar with her first job, and her daughter, who is no longer a child, no longer feels the need to talk about it. And yet she is still very keen to see the salon – or, if it no longer exists, the place where it used to be.

It is a chilly yet bright September morning. Clara, who doesn't have any meetings at the theatre until midday, has a couple of hours to spare, and deep down, she is in the same mind as Isabella. She has never been back to Chalon: the opportunity has never arisen. Her parents live in the Morvan, her sister in Louhans and her friend Anaïs has gone to live in Lisbon. She's only come back for the show this evening.

She calls the hotel in case they are expecting them, then she walks down Boulevard de la République with her daughter. They turn left at the end, towards the citadel. The salon wasn't far from here. Isabella, who is accustomed to the bustle of Parisian life, responds the way she does every time she gets away from it. She finds everything charming, cosy; she hasn't even been there for ten minutes when she starts talking about spending some time here after her baccalaureate. Clara, who is paying close attention to the evolution of the city, notes that not much has changed. The shops, maybe a little. A Fnac has opened on Rue du Général-Leclerc, and it seems that the people of Chalon now eat only tacos and kebabs. But the city's personality, which she thinks of as being like a Resistance fighter against the tides of ugliness and greed, a soldier who might be better off if they were less alone, seems to her unchanged.

On Avenue de Paris, she catches sight of a poster for a show in the most recent edition of 'Chalon in the Street', a Jean-Marc Reiser–style drawing that sends her back to the past just as powerfully as hearing a record for the first time in years. It all comes back to her: the little rattan stool, the rugs that Anaïs helped her carry and the list of readings taped just underneath the no-entry sign; and she realises that her daughter doesn't know very much about that period in her life – about her whirlwind love affair with Proust, the significance of his book for her, the transition he enabled her to make from the world she had so far inhabited to the world of art and artists – the only world, ultimately, that could ever have made her life interesting. She'll have to tell her about it, have to talk about those slightly crazy few months during which Clara felt like she was running ever faster, taking a run-up and then leaping as far as she could. How else will she understand why her mother has devoted her life to making great texts heard – or in other words, to spending every evening trying to get others to experience the sense of wonder that she felt upon reading *In Search of Lost Time*?

It is an inspiring story. Not all that many people reinvent themselves. We usually take the version of reality that we are first presented with and refrain from questioning it because we don't dare to, because it is easier and more comfortable, and, in doing so, we live out the imperfect, frustrating life of someone who only resembles us from afar. Not much is certain about this life, and it is only becoming less so, but there is this: we don't realise the extent to which our fates have been shaped by others.

Once they get to Place de la Libération, they pause so Clara can get her bearings. The pharmacy she sees wasn't there before; it has replaced the café on the corner that was run by the platinum blonde who would come and visit them when they opened, and whose name escapes her.

'The salon was down this passage,' she says, gesturing towards it. 'On the left-hand side.'

Isabella raises an eyebrow – an expression she has inherited from her father. 'It's a strange place to have it. Not very busy.'

'You're right; it was strange having this little salon hidden away down here when there were other ones on the square in full view. Plus, it was set back in the passage; people couldn't see it. I don't think my boss was very business-minded.'

'What happened to her?'

Clara thinks back to a phone call from her mother two or three years previously perhaps, after she'd left Chalon. Annick had read in *Le Journal de Saône-et-Loire* about a woman who'd met her end on the road to Tournus while making a call at the wheel of her Mini Mayfair. *Wasn't Madame Habib the name of your old boss?*

She is about to reply to her daughter, but she doesn't get the chance. They have gone down the passage and Isabella has spotted the little nook and gone ahead, eager to find out whether the salon is still there. When she comes to a halt, Clara can hardly believe what she sees.

It is still a hair salon, with the small glass door on the left and the same window display just beside it, concealing nothing of what's inside. But this place is called *L'Hair du temps*, the walls are a pale green, the décor is minimalist, and it doesn't have a counter now. And the staff has changed, of course. Just one hairdresser, probably the owner, is half sitting behind a teenager while she shaves the back of his neck. She is rather stocky, in her forties, and has short hair. Clara thinks she recognises her. Yes, it *is* her – it's Nolwenn, sixteen years older. She senses that someone is out in the passage and looks to the left. She sees Clara and then quickly turns away again. She didn't recognise her. She adjusts her glasses and says something to the teenager, who smiles back at her. And just when Clara has told herself that things are probably better this way, that there are some memories that shouldn't be awakened, she sees Nolwenn look her way again, slowly this time. That woman outside the window . . . her face looks familiar.

Acknowledgements

To the Centre national du livre and the Région Bourgogne-Franche-Comté, who both awarded me grants to write this book.

And to Evelyne Bloch-Dano, Antoine Gallimard, Karina Hocine, Antoine Laurain, Laurent Mauvignier, Jean-Noël Pancrazi and Maud Simonnot for their invaluable support.